# A SECRET TO DIE FOR
By Cynthia Hickey

# CHAPTER ONE

Darcie Thayer's legs wobbled as fear choked her.

She didn't want to run anymore. Life didn't matter. What they'd do to her before they killed her scared Darcie the most. Once they had what Tony had hid, they'd have no further need of her.

She stared at the quaint town spread in a kaleidoscope-pattern a thousand feet below. She couldn't find a safe place. Not even a small town in the middle of nowhere, Arkansas would provide the refuge she sought. Especially not this place. But, she had run out of options.

Grasping the want ads with her right hand, she clutched the fence rail constructed to keep the Ozark Mountain tourists from plunging to their deaths. Despite her queasiness of heights, Darcie wished she were a bird that could soar at will.

The wind grabbed the paper and sent it twisting

and twirling off to the valley below. Her cotton skirt whipped around her knees, and she swayed forward. She stumbled back, her heart in her throat.

Lightning shot across the sky like the tentacles of an octopus. The air crackled with electricity. Thunder crashed. Darcie lifted the long peasant-style skirt above her knees and sprinted for her '69 Chevy Impala. She hated the car. Detested it really, but she'd lost everything when Tony died. Money, home, security, car…and her unborn child. This monstrous boat was all she owned.

Her hand rubbed across her stomach as she envisioned the baby she'd carried. She stopped beside the car and lifted her face to heaven to let the rain wash away her guilt. The sky grumbled louder. She ducked and yanked the vehicle door open and scrambled inside.

Tony had promised her a new life. One filled with hope. With promise. Empty promises. One selfish act and her world lay shattered at her feet like a bashed mirror. The future didn't seem worth pursuing.

Her grandmother's voice emerged from the recesses of her mind. "Don't worry about tomorrow. Today has enough problems of its own." If so, then reliving the past was just as much a waste of time.

"Now what?" Darcie asked her reflection in the rearview mirror. "I've lost the address to my new job. All I know is the guy's name. York Wardell. An author who wants a live-in nanny to care for his kids. Probably while he writes the next great American novel." She scoffed and brushed wet bangs from her face. "Well, ready or not, here I come. Somebody around here is bound to know where the guy lives."

The drive down the mountain, with thunder booming around her, left Darcie's hands white-knuckled and shaking. She glanced at her watch and groaned. An hour late. She'd told the man she'd arrive for dinner. They'd agreed it would be a perfect time for her to get acquainted with the children. Would her new boss buy her excuse that she got lost?

She maneuvered her four-wheeled monstrosity into the first fast food drive-through she came to. Along with placing an order for a hamburger and fries, she asked the kid behind the window whether he knew of a York Wardell.

"Sure. He coaches the high school football team. At least until they get someone else hired." The pimply-faced youth pointed west and spouted off a list of directions as twisting as a country road.

"Thanks. I think I'll find it." Darcie peeled rubber out of the parking lot and headed in the direction of yet another mountain. "Great," she mumbled around a mouthful of ground beef. "It's getting dark, it's raining, and I've got to find this guy's house during a storm. Can life get any better?"

She'd almost made it to the top when her tire blew. Darcie stomped the brakes and sent the car into a skid. She dropped her hamburger.

Which way were you supposed to steer? Into the skid or away? Left? Right? She decided on left and jerked the wheel.

The Impala fishtailed on the wet blacktop. The steel divider between the road and emptiness loomed. Her stomach plunged like Niagra Falls. A scream ripped free of her throat.

The car skid along the rail. Metal against metal screeched as piercing as a siren. She closed her eyes and prayed even though she'd convinced herself God no longer cared.

The car finally shuddered to a stop. Darcie cut the ignition and slammed against the door. Locked. Pain radiated up her shoulder. After a few more lunges and grasping of slippery fingers on the lock, she got the door open and slid from the seat.

She slipped through the mud as she circled the car to check for damage. The passenger side sported a curved-in wide swatch of unpainted metal.

"And I thought you were ugly before." Darcie sniffed and leaned against the hood. "Now what do I do?"

She folded her arms across her chest, stared into the dark sky, and blinked against the falling drops. "Did you hear me, God? What do I do now? Could you maybe make it rain harder? How about some closer lightning? You know how much I love storms."

The sky lit in a brilliant display of fire. Darcie dove inside the car.

Rain pounded the roof, deafening in its ferocity. She wrapped her arms around her middle, hoping to find warmth. She sulked, shivered, and yelled. At God. When her watch showed ten o'clock, she grabbed her purse, suitcase, and keys, then exited into a drizzle.

Her feet slipped in her wet sandals. The sodden skirt tangled around her legs. Thighs trembling from the uphill climb, she stopped before collapsing in a soggy heap beside the road.

*It's too soon. I'm not ready to begin life again. A year wasn't enough. I need five years. Ten years.* The ever-present risk of danger hovered over her. How could she subject someone else's family to potential threat? Hiding on top of a mountain didn't guarantee they wouldn't find her. Especially since they'd come for her at the hospital. She shrugged. Finding what her husband had hid was top priority. She'd do whatever it took.

Darcie wrapped her arms around her knees and clenched her chattering teeth. Where did she go from here? Farther up apparently, but the clouds covered the moon and stars. She sat in darkness.

The drizzle finally stopped. Sounds seemed magnified. Not being a country girl since she'd left home at eighteen, Darcie's heart beat an unnatural rhythm every time the woods around her popped, splashed, or snapped. *You've got to move, girl. If you don't, you'll be a bear's dinner.*

With that encouraging thought, she rose and continued. Blisters formed between her toes from the prong of the sandals. Her temper smoldered, and her rolling suitcase weighed five hundred pounds. She stumbled on a rock, stubbing her toe. Pain shot through her foot, and she gasped.

Headlight beams sliced through the night. Darcie squinted and raised a hand to shield her eyes.

The truck, an older model, passed. Water sprayed from its tires. drenching her further. Darcie gritted her teeth and turned to glare. She ought to do more than stare. Flee, in case the truck held her pursuers. But exhaustion hovered just under the surface.

Relief mingled with fear flooded her body as the vehicle turned back in her direction. Too tired to care, Darcie collapsed. Let them kill her.

The Ford stopped. Its beams dimmed. The driver-side door opened, and a cowboy boot-covered foot emerged to plant firmly on the ground. Darcie allowed her gaze to travel up the denim-clad legs as the man stepped in front of the lights. He towered above her. Her heart accelerated.

"Are you all right?" A rich baritone swept over her. The apparent knight in shining truck knelt before her.

Darcie glanced into dark eyes framed by wire-rimmed glasses. The eyes were set into the most handsome face she'd ever seen. A face so good-looking, it should only appear on the pages of a magazine. Her breath caught. She had to be hallucinating.

"Miss?"

She shook her head to clear it. "I've had an accident."

"You wouldn't be Darcie Thayer by any chance, would you?" He placed a hand beneath her elbow and helped her to her feet.

"York Wardell?" This couldn't be her boss. Luck didn't run that way for her. Or maybe it did. What a wonderful way to meet a new employer. Wet and bedraggled.

"The one and only. Where's your car?"

"About a mile back with a flat tire."

York led her to the passenger side of the pickup. "I'll take you to the house. We'll pick up your car tomorrow."

Darcie folded her arms and sank back into the seat. "I got lost. Then I got the flat tire and almost went sailing off the mountain. I apologize for being late."

"The kids have gone to bed. The housekeeper is watching them." He glanced at her. "You'll have to meet them tomorrow."

"It was really out of my control."

A muscle twitched in his jaw. "It's fine."

Okay, how fitting. A beautiful face with a nasty attitude. Her spirit sank. She wanted Tony back. Faults and all. At least they'd understood each other.

~

"The main thing is, you're okay. " She looked like a drowned rat and--in spite of himself, York felt a tug on his heart as he stared at her. She looked too young to be a nanny. She'd said twenty-eight, but he swore she couldn't be older than nineteen. Red hair hung limp around a face with sparkling golden eyes and just a sprinkle of freckles across her nose.

When he'd driven past and noticed her slumped like a lump on the side of the road, he'd thought at first she was injured. After he discovered she'd only been stupid enough to walk in the dark, he'd felt the first stirrings of anger—at himself for feeling pity and for her—he shrugged. No reason to be mad at her. It was nothing but bad timing with a flat tire.

It didn't help that she was pretty, despite her drenching. After Michelle's betrayal, the last thing he needed, or wanted, was to entertain thoughts of another woman. He definitely didn't need a tiny slip of a woman complicating things. And York knew his weaknesses. The major one: a pretty face or a damsel in distress.

"How did you know where to find me?" Darcie swiped wet hair out of her face.

"There's only one road on and off this mountain unless you drive all the way around. It wasn't hard."

"Oh." Her hand cradled her stomach, almost protectively, as she glanced behind them.

"Are you hurt? Sick? Looking for someone?" York peered in the rearview mirror.

"No, why?" Darcie straightened.

"Just wondering." She'd touched her stomach the way Michelle had when she was pregnant with Sam and Sarah. *Please don't let her be pregnant.* There isn't exactly a cornucopia of nannies in this part of the state. And, forgive him, Lord, but he had a deadline to meet.

York sighed. When had he gotten so mean? When Michelle died, that's when. With someone new living in the house, he vowed to work on his attitude.

They made the rest of the drive in silence. Occasionally, she'd shiver and wrap her arms tightly around her middle. York's gut clenched as sympathy for her increased. He ought to be more compassionate. Isn't that what the Bible taught? "I'm sorry I don't have a blanket or jacket, but we'll be home soon. Have you eaten?"

"Yes, thank you. I grabbed a burger when I stopped for directions. I'm sorry for the inconvenience. I really appreciate you coming to look for me." Darcie turned to face him. "I'll have breakfast ready by seven a.m., and the children dropped off at school by eight. If I can borrow a car, that is. Then what do I do?"

"Whatever you want. Cooking isn't part of your job description. I have a housekeeper. You'll be free until you pick the kids up at three. School is out in a week. You'll be plenty busy then."

"Great." She stared into the side mirror.

"Are you sure you aren't looking for someone?" Car lights pierced the night behind them.

"Positive. I'm just tired."

She sounded obstinate, her voice soft, yet hard as steel. York struggled to keep from smiling. He'd have difficulty taking such a small thing serious if she got really angry. Like a furious forest sprite. He'd known the woman five minutes, and she'd already shown she had two sides to her.

Two sides that traded places faster than a tornado could blow apart a trailer park. But, could she handle a couple of hurricanes named Sam and Sarah?

# CHAPTER TWO

Darcie woke to two pairs of chocolate brown eyes staring at her. For a moment, she forgot where she was and pulled the blankets to her chin. The stares disconcerted her, and she wished she could pull the covers higher.

"Are you our new nanny?" A little girl with shoulder-length mahogany curls, and eyes as large as dinner plates studied Darcie. An older boyish version stood next to her.

"Yes. I'm Darcie. Do you usually just waltz into a stranger's room?"

"She's Miss Thayer to you two." York paused in the open doorway. "Now, leave Miss Thayer in peace so she can get out of bed."

Privacy seemed in short supply in this house. Well, she'd put a stop to that quick enough. Tonight, she'd lock her door. Darcie raised her gaze.

York's eyes were the same as the children's. Not

black as she'd thought last night. Pools of dark chocolate framed by gold-rimmed glasses. Raven curls swept back from a high forehead. A cleft in his chin. A smirk on chiseled lips. Definitely pretty. She dropped her gaze to the muscled biceps beneath a black tee shirt. Pretty, but all man.

"It's eight o'clock." He frowned and gave a nod toward the clock on the nightstand.

"Oh." Darcie started to toss aside the blankets, then remembered the thin cotton nightgown she'd slept in. "I'm sorry. I'll be right down."

York gave another almost imperceptible nod and motioned for the children to follow him out of the room.

How could she sleep late on her first day? Mr. Wardell must think her a total waste of time. First last night and now this. He probably wondered why he'd hired her.

Lacking a long list of references, Darcie had practically begged the man to give her a chance. York seemed like the last resort to the beginning of a new life. With a sigh, she threw aside the covers and dangled her legs over the bed. She stared around her.

Containing only the full-size bed she slept in, and a single dresser free of dust and ornamentation, the room was clean, but lacked the touch a woman could give. Neutral-colored blinds covered the window. Maybe he'd let her personalize her space. The wooden boards on the floor shone with a high sheen and the linens crackled with freshness.

"I'm glad he's got a maid." She didn't want to be the one to clean the place.

An image of a massive log cabin loomed before her. The night before, she'd stared in awe at the impressive structure that towered over them like a giant beast, then allowed herself to be ushered inside and to bed. Now to start her new job.

She didn't have a clue how to entertain kids. Fake credentials and a lot of smooth talking got her here. The man must have been desperate to hire someone. Darcie stood. Has anyone fed the children? She flung open her suitcase, then snagged a pair of blue jeans and a deep-purple tank top. She hadn't thought to ask whether the Wardell household required dress regulations.

Darcie buried her face in her hands. She wasn't cut out for this. Until Tony's death, she hadn't had to work. He'd made plenty of money. Sales, he told her whenever she asked. She snorted. She knew the truth, now. From that horrific moment on, she'd done nothing but work. Odd jobs here and there. Mostly waitressing. But nanny? Never in her wildest dreams.

Cheerful chatter led her to the kitchen where Sam and Sara sat with cereal in front of them. The children stopped talking when she entered, watching her with impassive faces.

"Good morning." Darcie's voice shook. Was she afraid? Of two children? She'd faced worse.

Sarah smiled. "Good morning."

Sam shoveled food in his mouth with gusto, avoiding her gaze and staring into his bowl.

Spotting a pot of coffee on the counter and a clean mug beside it, Darcie practically ran toward her morning fuel. One sip told her Mr. Wardell didn't skimp on his coffee grounds. She practically moaned with pleasure.

"That all you gonna eat?" Sam's drawl was so thick, Darcie thought he spoke another language.

"*Is* this all I'm going to eat? Yes." She stepped over and pulled out a chair across the table from Sam and Sarah.

Sam pushed his empty bowl away. "Are you another of them ladies who care how a kid talks? Ain't that what teachers are for?"

"I talk good." Sarah dropped her spoon with a clatter.

This wouldn't be easy. Darcie sipped slowly from her mug before answering. "You're right. I'm not a teacher. I've never taken language classes. But I have grown up in the South, and I was taught to speak like a lady. Intelligently. You don't want people to think you're stupid, do you?"

"I ain't stupid!" The boy folded his arms.

"Then don't speak like you are." Darcie rose. Their father was an author. Why didn't he teach the children proper grammar? "It's time for me to get you to school. You're going to be late. I'm sorry."

The children grabbed backpacks from the floor near the table and darted outside. When Darcie turned, she spotted York leaning against the kitchen wall, face expressionless, muscular arms crossed. Her steps faltered. She recovered and strode after Sam and Sarah.

Would he be upset at her for correcting his son? She didn't know how else to deal with children except for the way her dear grandma raised her. With firmness, offset with kindness.

Sam and Sarah waited beside the same pickup York drove the night before. A fairly new model, king-cab Ford painted navy blue.

Darcie slapped her forehead. "I've forgotten the keys."

"They're in the glove box." Sam yanked open the door and climbed into the front passenger seat, leaving the back for his little sister.

"Are you allowed to ride up here?" Darcie slid behind the wheel. "You aren't twelve and there's no way to turn off the air bags."

"Yes."

"No, he isn't," Sarah piped up.

"In the back, Sam." Darcie retrieved the keys. "Isn't your father afraid someone will steal his truck?"

"Out here?" Sam joined his sister, making a great show of buckling his seatbelt. "Nothing happens this far out of town."

"Right." Darcie started the motor, and then wheeled the Ford around in the wide gravel driveway. "How silly of me."

There wasn't a sound from the children until Darcie drove past her car sitting forlornly on the side of the otherwise empty road. Sam laughed.

"That must be yours. We don't get much traffic up here. You must think you're in hog-heaven driving this after that thing."

"It's not very pretty, is it?" Sarah's voice joined her brother's.

"No, it isn't. But it's all I have. You shouldn't make fun."

"Just being honest." Several minutes later, Sam

asked, "Do you even know where to go?"

"I'm relying on you to tell me. A big boy of ten should know how to get to his school."

"Turn right once you get off the mountain."

"You turn left. Stop lying, Sam."

"Thank you, Sarah." Darcie turned left. "Now where?"

"Drive straight. When you have to stop again, take another left. You'll see the school."

Following Sarah's instructions, they arrived at their destination ten minutes later. "Thank you again." Darcie smiled at the girl as she climbed from the truck. "I knew where to go. Just checking to see whether Sam would be honest."

Sam slid out his side and stopped beside her window. "Do you think you can find your way back at three?"

"I think so." Obviously, the children and she would play a power game for a while. One she vowed to win.

"You have to come sign us in since we're late." Sam crossed his arms.

"Oh. Right." Please don't let anyone she knew still be working here.

Coming home was a bad idea. But desperation did that to a person. Even sending them to the last place they wanted to be in order to find something they weren't sure was hidden where it could be found. Her shoulders sagged.

Darcie waited for Sam to move so she could open her door enough to get out. He smirked and stepped out the way.

Her luck ran its usual course. Behind the counter

sat one of the women who used to be in the 'popular group' in high school. A girl Darcie had loved to hate. Darcie forced her lips into a smile.

"Why if it isn't Darcie McGee! What brings you back here?" The woman held her ash blond hair in place with a sparkling headband. Thick waves brushed her shoulders. Her smile didn't reach the pale blue eyes studying Darcie.

"It's Darcie Thayer now. Hello, Suzy." There's no way she'd tell this woman she'd moved home to hide. The back of Darcie's neck prickled. She glanced toward the front of the building. The glass blocks allowed in sunlight, but didn't provide a clear view to the outside.

The woman stood. "That's right. You married Tony. Shadow Springs' bad boy. How is he?"

Sam and Sarah's gazes swept back and forth between the women, their expressions full of questions.

"Tony's dead." Darcie's heart clenched. "A year now. Are you married yet? As I recall, you had plenty of boys chasing you."

Suzy gave the smallest shake of her head. Her cheeks flushed pink beneath her makeup.

Darcie reached for the pen beside the clipboard on the counter. "I'm the Wardells's new nanny. You must be the school secretary. As a student, I always thought school secretaries were old."

"Times change." Suzy's smile faded. "You're here to stay?"

"That's right." Darcie flashed the woman a grin, enjoying her obvious dismay. "At least for now."

"I haven't been back in town long myself. Are

you staying at the cabin?"

"Don't nannies usually stay with the children in their care?"

Suzy transferred her attention to Sam and Sarah. "Y'all go to class." Without turning back to Darcie, she took the clipboard. "Welcome back."

Darcie suspected Suzy didn't mean the words of welcome. She spun and marched back to the truck.

That had gone easier than she'd thought. Her first meeting with someone from her past, and her high-school nemesis to boot. It would get easier. . .with time. But time wasn't a plentiful resource. Not unless she wanted to meet Tony's fate.

She stepped into sunshine. A dark sedan with tinted windows backed out of the parking space beside the truck. Darcie's heart stuttered. She mentally shook herself. Probably a parent dropping off a late student like she had. She straightened her shoulders and marched forward, pausing at the scrap of white paper on the windshield.

With a trembling hand, she freed it from beneath the wiper blade and read:

Give us the list or suffer the consequences.

~

York couldn't help but be impressed as he watched Darcie load the children in the Ford. Sam had steadily become more of a trial since his mother's death. The red-haired forest sprite handled him well. He'd tried correcting his son's grammar, but even that got too hard.

After she'd stalked out behind the kids, York climbed the stairs to his study. He'd drawn the floor plan to suit his needs, building his office under an eave with large windows that let in plenty of the Southern summer sun.

He'd debated about whether he should've built the cabin over the foundation of the old home. The view from his land made the decision for him. From his window, he looked over the town below. The surrounding farms added color to the rich emerald of the trees.

The computer monitor beckoned. His agent had reached the screaming point, demanding York finish his latest manuscript by the end of the summer. Only problem was his muse had deserted him. Now, distraction in the form of a strawberry-haired whip of a girl complicated matters even more. He sensed she hid something. Nothing he could put his finger on, but there all the same. She'd definitely been watching out the truck window last night. Almost as if she expected to be followed.

He sighed and fell into the plush leather office chair. The words on the screen ran together in a pattern of freckles and curly hair. He laid his head against the back of the chair. What was with him and women?

Allowing Michelle to dictate how much time he spent writing had been a huge mistake. Then she'd died, and he had the manner of her death to deal with. Now, a pretty woman invaded his thoughts. Stupid.

The front door banged open, hitting the wall in the room below. He'd promised to fix the doorstop, but time ran on faster than he did. Other things seemed more important.

"Sorry!"

He cringed at the shouted word. York counted on the hours the children were at school to be silent and undisturbed enough for him to write. He prayed the newest nanny in a long line of nannies, wouldn't cause more distraction than his children.

What had he been thinking hiring a woman so young and obviously inexperienced? She didn't fit the mold of his prior nannies. No matter how knowledgeable the women had been, the children managed to run off every one.

Trying to refocus on the words of his latest true-crime novel, he poised his fingers over the keyboard.

A glass shattered. The crash seemed to come from the direction of the kitchen.

"Sorry!"

"Wish I was a swearing man." York ran his fingers through his hair.

# CHAPTER THREE

Boredom forced Darcie upstairs. It hadn't taken long to clean up the shattered mug, nor wipe down the counters and put away the children's breakfast dishes. York hadn't said anything to her about cleaning, but as a maid had yet to make an appearance, and a lack of activity left Darcie anxious, she decided to explore the upper portion of the house.

She supposed she could set out to find Tony's hidden package, but the mood hadn't struck. If she put it off long enough, maybe it'd go away. Life could be good, right? Other people seemed content, even happy. Why not her? She didn't want to keep people at bay with a bristling personality. She thirsted for companionship. When things were safe. Then, she'd pursue the life she dreamed of.

A long hallway ran at the top of the steps with rooms branching off each side. A tall window allowed light in at the far end. Darcie headed in that direction.

The view took her breath away. The same view from the overlook of the previous night. Protection of the glass allowed her to look at her leisure without the fear of taking that step over the edge.

A solid canopy of oak and pine spread below her, directing an observer's eye to the valley. In the distance, she imagined she could see the house where she'd grown up. A house filled with terror more than love. Until her grandmother rescued her. Now, she'd have to go back for something Tony had left behind.

With a deep sigh, she turned and opened the nearest door. The perfect little girl's sanctuary. The walls a delicate pink with white wainscoting half way up. A canopy bed fit for a princess was the focal point of the room. Blankets hung halfway off and puddled on the floor.

Darcie stepped around discarded dolls and fuzzy animals and made her way to the bed. She pulled the blankets into place and smoothed them over the mattress. She gathered the stuffed animals and leaned them against the mound of pillows. Within minutes, she'd tossed the other toys into a wooden chest.

She moved to Sam's room next. NASCAR posters adorned the midnight blue walls. The blankets on his twin bed lay in a pile on the floor. She had just finished pulling the coverings in place when York stopped in the doorway.

"Sam and Sarah are in charge of cleaning their own messes."

Darcie shrugged. "It's no problem, really."

"I insist. They won't learn responsibility if someone is making their beds and cleaning up their toys."

"I'm sorry. I didn't know. Right now, I'm just trying to win them over and keep myself from going stir crazy."

"Sam can be a challenge." He bent and picked up a book. "Sarah will be easier. The trick will be keeping Sam from influencing her."

Darcie sat on the edge of the bed. "It must be hard for him. A boy misses his mother too." She glanced around. There wasn't a single picture of a woman who could be his mother. None of his father, either. "How did she die?"

"Fire." York turned on his heel and stormed away.

The room chilled. She had obviously hit a sore spot. She shrugged. It wasn't any of her business. Her employer made that as clear as a sparkling mountain stream. Keeping her distance from the brooding man seemed the safe choice.

One last toss of a football into the closet, and she took one last look around, then left. Another door revealed a bathroom with damp towels left on the floor and a toothpaste tube without a lid. The urge to clean left her after York's curt dismissal. She turned. She might as well complete her snooping.

The master bedroom. Masculine, cold, bare of decorative touches. She closed the door as if her fingers could catch fire from the knob.

The last room revealed Mr. Author himself standing at a window, staring out, his hands clasped behind his back. He didn't turn around. "This is my study. Off limits if the door is closed."

"Sorry. I. . .I was wondering?"

"Yes?" He turned and focused a hard stare on her.

"Do you have a maid? I mean, I know you said you had a housekeeper, but. . ."

"Excuse me?"

Darcie gripped the door handle hard enough to cause the knob to dig into her hand. "A maid. I just noticed things were getting dusty, and, well. . .I don't like to be bored, so I wondered…"

"Feel free. It's not included in your pay. You're being paid to meet my children's needs. Not the house's."

"Are you always this unfriendly?" She wished she could have stopped the words. Too late.

He stiffened. His lips disappeared in a thin line.

"I'll leave now." She couldn't get out fast enough. She almost expected him to come after her and terminate her services. Her grandmother had always told her to hold her tongue. That someday it would get her in trouble. What was that Bible verse her grandma always quoted? Something about the tongue being a raging fire.

Should she ask him to borrow the truck? To help her get her car? Darcie scoffed. She'd rather eat peas.

~

What did he want from life? York didn't know. Happiness? Love? Or did he want to be left alone? God knew he had tried the love angle and that worked out less than great.

The front door slammed, followed by the sound of his truck roaring from the driveway. He didn't blame her. He'd acted abominably. He knew better. He'd been unfriendly, rude, even, and he hadn't managed to write a single word.

Her question about Michelle's death cut deep. York still couldn't bring himself to tell anyone that his wife hadn't been alone when she died in the fire. The investigators discovered another body alongside hers. A man's. They'd found the remains in the master bedroom. Along with a shattered whiskey bottle.

Still, five years later, the knowledge of his wife's unfaithfulness ate at him like a cancer. Burrowed to his bones. Writing a novel that had once taken just months to research and finish, now took almost a year. Or more.

Maybe he should've moved. Packed up the kids and moved west. But, he couldn't bring himself to leave their home. He'd lived in Shadow Springs since high school. When he'd met a raven-haired beauty named Michelle.

He fell into his chair with enough force to almost tip backward. The two of them had had a rollercoaster relationship. On again. Off again. His parents warned him that trying to tame Michelle would be like taming a tiger. They'd been right. He saw her every time he looked into the faces of his children. He'd failed his marriage, and now he was failing his children.

He kicked back from his desk, propelling himself into a bookcase. Paperbacks toppled to the floor. He wouldn't be writing today.

York marched down the stairs and strode out the front door, taking the road down the mountain. He'd walk to her car and drive it home. If Darcie hadn't left the keys in the ignition, he'd hotwire it. It was the least he could do after the way he'd treated her. Only natural for a person to wonder about the children they cared for.

When he reached her car, he stopped. No sight of the woman and he'd need his truck and tools to change the tire.

The sun beat on his head. The air hung heavy with humidity. Soon, his shirt clung to his back. He lifted his face to catch the slight breeze and continued to the overlook. Darcie stood staring over the edge. For a moment, his heart clinched. For a split-second, he thought she contemplated jumping.

His steps crunched on gravel. She turned and smiled. A sad, ghost of a smile, and he doubly regretted his behavior in his study. He'd been a jerk. Relating to another woman wouldn't come easy, but he vowed to try.

"Did you come to apologize?" She stepped away from the rail.

"Yes." York shoved his hands in his pockets.

"Hard for you, isn't it?"

"Yes."

"You don't talk much, do you?" She made her way over and stood before him.

Her head just reached his chin. A perfect height for him to rest upon. What was he thinking? "No, I don't."

"Wow. Three words in a row." She crossed her arms. "Let's hear it. Your apology."

"I did." He stiffened.

"No, you didn't. Try it. Two little words. Say, I'm sorry. You can do it."

The little minx. "I'm sorry. I was out of line and rude beyond the realms of courtesy. Better?"

"Much."

"I came to help you get your car to the house."

"Nice of you. But, I don't have a spare tire."

"We'll tow it."

Darcie turned and made her way to the truck. "How can an author be a man of such few words?"

"I use them all in my novels." He slid into the driver's seat before she had a chance. "We'd better get a move on if you're going to pick up the kids on time. We'll get your car on the way back."

Darcie glanced at a little gold strap of a watch. "It's two-thirty. Want to get a soda in town first?"

He hadn't been to town with a woman since Michelle. The thought didn't appeal to him, yet he surprised himself by saying yes. Darcie's face lit brighter than the summer sun and warmed his insides.

She chattered non-stop all the way down the mountain. He got a feeling the woman craved adult companionship. Well, she looked at the wrong man to fill that particular need.

Great. Parked in front of the local Tastee Freez sat a familiar red Mustang convertible. He hoped there was another one in town. No such luck. Suzy Bouchee's white hair shone through the front window. "Let's go somewhere else."

Darcie frowned. "There isn't anywhere else. At least not with such a varied menu. Not in this town."

"How do you know that?"

"I grew up here."

York stared at her, recognition striking him like a blow to the head. "I thought you looked familiar. Did we go to the same high school?"

"Yep, you were the all-star quarterback. A senior when I was a freshman. Girls followed you in droves. Especially one with long dark hair."

"Michelle. My late wife." He hadn't spoken those words aloud in years. "You didn't follow me, though."

"I didn't chase boys."

"They chased you?"

"Not really."

"Hard to believe."

"Believe what you want." She flung her door open and stormed into the diner. "Boys don't swarm after white trash."

Every time he opened his mouth he said the wrong thing. York sighed and followed. His first impression of her as a woman with two sides proved true.

When he entered, Darcie and Suzy glared at each other. Pit bulls. Snarling and growling.

The scowl magically disappeared from Suzy's face when she turned to greet him. "York! What a pleasure seeing you here."

"Aren't you supposed to be at work?" Darcie pushed past her and chose a booth in the corner. She turned back to York, one eyebrow raised.

"Not that it's any of your business, but I took the rest of the day off. Had some personal errands to run." Suzy placed a red-taloned hand on York's arm. "It paid off. You haven't called me."

"Obviously, I'm the third wheel here." Darcie exited the booth. "I'll walk on to the school. See you there, *Mister* York."

"Wait." He reached toward her, only to have Suzy claim his hand.

"Have a soda with me." Her cooing tone set his nerves on edge. "The kids won't be out of school for another fifteen minutes."

He shook free of her grasp. "Not this time, Suzy. Give me a rain check." Due in a million years.

He darted out the door and after the furiously marching Darcie. What had he done now? You'd think he'd forgotten how to act with a woman.

# CHAPTER FOUR

Darcie leaned against the red brick of the school building, one leg bent and balanced on the wall behind her. It surprised her York didn't erupt into flames from the heat of her stare. Employee or not, she expected more courtesy. She sighed, knowing she hadn't shown him any more than he'd given her.

Instead of grace, she'd acted like a jealous shrew over a man she knew less than twenty-four hours. If it had been anyone but Suzy, she'd have shrugged the whole thing off.

A dark sedan with tinted windows slowed in front of the diner then cruised past. Darcie took a deep breath to jump-start her stuttering heart. Hadn't she seen it before? Surely there was more than one dark car in Shadow Springs. How long until she stopped tensing at every unknown automobile that cruised past?

York jogged past the truck and across the

street, slowing his pace a few feet from her. "Hey, I thought we were having a soda. What's wrong? You look like you've seen a ghost."

"Must be the heat." Were men really that dense? "I changed my mind." Darcie turned her attention to the parking lot. She'd rather look at anything but him.

What really bothered her was how upset his knowing Suzy made her. It was none of her business whether the man knew Suzy. And from the woman's actions, it seemed they knew each other very well. Her boss had every right to speak to whomever he pleased. Just not her past nemesis. Please.

All during high school Suzy chased after whatever it seemed Darcie wanted. Not that she wanted York. She shook her head. No way. There wasn't room in her life for another man. Not even a handsome author who fit the tall, dark, quiet, and dangerous description to a T. That described Mr. Wardell.

Despite the obvious distinction in family status, Suzy, Shadow Springs' popular rich girl, and Darcie, offspring of the town drunk and a woman with loose morals, their paths had crossed too often during their teenage years to enable Darcie to be comfortable anywhere around the woman. Tony had been the only boy the other girl couldn't steal away. Darcie sighed and crossed her arms. Even he hadn't been what she'd thought.

"Okay." York leaned against the wall beside her. "We'll take the kids with us instead. Maybe grab some burgers. It's been a while since I've done that."

"Sure." Darcie snuck a peek from the corner of her eye.

The man was extraordinarily good-looking. His hair blew in the slight breeze, sticking in disarray all over his head. The gold-rimmed glasses only served to accent his eyes. The lips, well, she'd rather not go there. He definitely didn't look like her pre-conceived ideas of what an author should looklike. Bookish and plain.

Her love for Tony, if love was what she'd really felt for him, had been full of fear. The man hid a lot of secrets. One of which ultimately cost him his life.

But had he stirred her blood the way this stranger did? She sighed again. She didn't think so. York made her blood boil. In more ways than one.

"So, what's between you and Suzy?"

"Excuse me?" Darcie stiffened.

"I gathered you don't like her."

"I like her about as much as anyone can like a piranha." She gasped. "I'm sorry. I shouldn't have said that about your friend."

York laughed, the sound deep and rumbling up from his chest. He seemed like another man. One that didn't carry the weight of the world on his shoulders. "Suzy isn't my friend, although it isn't for lack of trying on her part. Piranha describes her very well."

"You appeared to enjoy the attention."

"She's an attractive lady." York stared at her. She squirmed beneath his scrutiny. "What man wouldn't be pleased with the attention?"

The dark sedan rolled past again. Darcie swallowed hard then turned to face the other direction. York glanced at her, then his gaze followed the car.

"Do you know them?"

"Nope." She forced a smile to her face. "Never saw that car before."

"Really, because you seem. . ."

Thankfully, the arrival of Sam and Sarah spared her having to answer. Smiles split the two children's faces at the sight of their father. Squeals pierced the air when he told them they were grabbing hamburgers from across the street.

Darcie grinned along with the Wardell family. How ordinary the outing seemed. Like a happy family. If only they were *her* family. Her hand moved to cover her flat stomach.

York's eyes widened. "Are you all right?"

"Yes, why?"

"I thought you might have a stomach ache. This isn't the first time I've noticed you covering your stomach."

"Nervous habit." She moved to walk ahead of him.

Suzy Boushee glared at them from her perch atop a barstool when the foursome entered the diner. Darcie raised her eyebrows and turned away, leading the rest to a corner booth. Let the woman shoot daggers at her. There'd been enough rivalry between them to last a lifetime. She didn't desire any more.

A teenage waitress skipped to their table, eager to take their order. She plopped down four glasses of ice water and promised to return in a couple of minutes.

Darcie picked up her menu and scanned the many ways someone could serve a hamburger, finally settling on a bacon cheeseburger. In the midst of Sarah's happy chatter, it took her a few minutes to notice the sullen look on Sam's face whenever his gaze fell on her.

The boy would answer his father's questions in one word. His gaze rarely left Darcie's face. Eventually, Sarah and her father seemed to pick up on the tension between the two. Conversation around the table became stilted. Smiles faded. York's gaze traveled from his son's face to Darcie's. His features settled into stone.

Instead of the friendly companionship Darcie had envisioned when he'd suggested dinner with the kids, the meal turned rushed. York paid the bill and with one hand gripping his son's arm, led them out the door and to the truck.

A muscle ticked in the corner of his mouth as he drove them back to Darcie's car. He barked orders for Sam to help him hitch the Impala to the truck, and despite Darcie's half-hearted attempts to tell him he acted unreasonable in regard to his son's feelings, they had a miserable drive home. She wanted nothing more than to crawl into a hole.

Once he'd turned off the truck's ignition, and shoved open his door, York stood as a silent, furious sentry until his son emerged and trudged into the house. "I'm sorry for my son's behavior."

A cold knot of uncertainty formed beneath Darcie's ribcage. Would the boy's obvious dislike of her be enough cause for York to fire her? Where would she go? She needed more time to find what Tony had hidden. "It's fine. It'll take him longer to adjust, that's all. I probably shouldn't have gone to eat with you. Just the three of you would've been better."

"Considering you'll be with them most of every day in a couple of weeks, he'd better start adjusting quickly. There was no excuse for his behavior. He'll be offering you an apology." York spun and stomped into the house, leaving a bewildered, yet relieved Darcie, on the front porch.

~

A stupid idea from the beginning. What had he been thinking to have the four of them go out for an early dinner? Even just for hamburgers? Of course, Sam would be disturbed. Darcie wasn't his mother. The children didn't want anyone else taking away what little of their father's attention they might receive.

Most of all, it'd been unfair to Darcie. York found himself coming too close to crossing the line between employer and something else. Friend, perhaps? Did he want to be her friend? Could he trust his feelings to another woman? Was he so starved for companionship he would accept the friendship of a woman in his employ?

His son's abominable behavior had ruined a perfectly good evening. Of course he'd have to apologize. York wouldn't make the same mistake over a woman again. Not even at the sight of sparkling amber eyes and dimples. Or the curvy body of a…He refused to go there. And what's up with her strange reaction to the car they'd seen outside the diner? She'd looked scared to death.

*God, what am I thinking? What are these thoughts in my head over a woman I've just met?*

"Samuel!"

His son slouched down the stairs and plopped on the bottom step. He tilted a belligerent face toward York.

"You will apologize to Mrs. Thayer."

"What for?"

"Your behavior at the diner was beyond rude."

"Why'd she have to go anyway? She's sticking her nose into our business." He folded his arms in an exact imitation of his father. "She's just hired help, Dad."

Seeing his son's posture and demeanor duplicating his, caused York to force himself to relax. He took a seat next to Sam and placed an arm around his son's shoulders. It'd been a long time since they'd had a heart-to-heart. The knowledge shot a stab of pain through his chest.

"Why don't you tell me what's really bothering you? I don't think this is solely about the new nanny."

He didn't think it was possible for Sam's shoulders to slump any lower. "The kids at school are saying bad things about Mom." A shudder passed through his body. "And now they're saying them about Mrs. Thayer."

An icy fist gripped York's heart. "What kind of things?"

"About Mom's dying in that fire. Jason, the fire chief's nephew said there was a man with her and that she was a drunk." Sam raised a tear-streaked face. "Now they're all saying the same thing is going to happen to you and Mrs. Thayer. That y'all are living in sin." He shrugged. "I punched the kid that said that one."

"We're not living in sin. Mrs. Olsen is here. She's been in and out because of her brother being ill, but she's made sure to be home every night." York sighed. "Mrs. Thayer isn't going to replace your mother, and," he ruffled his son's hair. "I think you and I are way past due for a fishing trip. The football team has that scrimmage game on Friday. We'll go fishing afterward and spend the night."

"What about your story?"

"I need a break." He'd gladly give up more than just writing time to keep that look of joy on his son's face. "Anyway, I think it's time we move on with our lives, don't you?" He wagged a finger in Sam's face. "No more punching. Violence is never the answer."

"Yeah, sure."

"Then how about giving Mrs. Thayer a break?"

"Okay. She ain't that bad, really. She cleaned my room." Sam jumped up and took the stairs two-at-a-time.

Comfort as welcoming as a mug of fresh roast warmed York. He'd be sure to make good on his promise of an outing with his son. Maybe invite Darcie and Sarah along too. An easy, relaxing way for them all to become better acquainted. Getting Sam to accept his new nanny would benefit everyone and result in a more peaceful home.

Somehow this slip of a woman could become

very important to the Wardell family. But, there was a story buried beneath the freckles. York intended to find out what it was. Why she kept looking over her shoulder.

His smile faded. Darcie stood framed in the front doorway, her face as pale as when he'd joined her outside the diner.

# CHAPTER FIVE

His wife had died in the arms of another man. The thought was horrible enough to push aside Darcie's heartache. Instead, pity for the man sitting on the stairs washed over her. Then, she noticed the look on his face. One that dared her to comment or show sympathy.

"Uh, well, I guess Sam will behave better for me now."

"I imagine so." York removed his glasses and pinched the bridge of his nose. He replaced the glasses and rose. "There's a practice football game Friday night, then a one-night camping trip. We'll all go." He opened his mouth as if to say something else but slumped his shoulders, turned, and climbed the stairs, leaning heavily on the banister.

She'd landed in a house of hurting people. How could she care for them when she could barely care for herself? When she struggled every day just to move forward? Her grandmother would've told her the fastest course to healing would be to help someone else. If only Darcie was strong enough.

Maybe there was something to the God her grandmother had believed in. Some powerful Being that knew more than the mere mortals who inhabited earth. She certainly hadn't done a good job of taking care of herself. Tired of running, Darcie had come back to the one place she'd vowed never to return. Sent there by a letter in the mail threatening her if she didn't find what Tony took.

She'd have to go to the shack where she'd suffered so much pain as a child to retrieve something Tony had stashed. She had no idea what to look for. Just whispered words from her dying husband about the hidden secret …something. His words failed him then. His eyes closed, and she became an injured widow clinging to a life she didn't want.

An empty evening full of loneliness loomed before her. Too early for the children to have their baths, and they didn't need her for that anyway. If she spent too much time alone, she worried the mountain overlook would call her with its siren song.

A book. She'd look for the friendliest person in the household to ask where York kept his books. He was an author, after all. He was bound to have several.

Darcie found Sarah in the kitchen, doodling on a piece of notebook paper. "What are you doing?"

The little girl jerked. "My homework?"

"Really?" Darcie peered at the squiggles and circles. "Art class?"

Sarah sighed. "No. I can't concentrate."

Darcie pulled up a chair and spent an enjoyable half hour helping Sarah with elementary math and spelling. Something she *could* do.

When Sarah put her completed homework in her backpack, Darcie smoothed the little girl's hair from her face. "How about some cookies?"

"We don't have any."

"We'll make some. I'm good at baking. You can help."

"I've never made cookies before." Sarah skipped to the counter and climbed on a bar stool.

"First, we need a big bowl. Can you find one?" Darcie sorted through the pantry, pulling out ingredients for cookies. She almost squealed with delight when she ran across a bag of chocolate chips.

"Mrs. Olsen sometimes brings us cookies, but we've never made them ourselves." Sarah clunked a glass bowl on the counter. "Sometimes she makes some for when we get home from school."

"Mrs. Olsen?"

"She's our maid. Her brother's sick, so she's been gone most of the day. Comes back here to sleep. It's way past dark by the time she shows up." Sarah dumped chocolate chips into the bowl.

"I mentioned a maid to your dad. He didn't give me a lot of information."

"Probably thought it wasn't any of your business." Sarah climbed back on the stool. "Or maybe he thought you wouldn't last long enough to meet her. That's probably it."

No way would she quit now. They wouldn't be

able to run her off with a chainsaw and hockey mask. Darcie dumped the rest of the ingredients into the bowl and forced a smile on her face.

She wouldn't allow thoughts of the Neanderthal upstairs to ruin what could be a lovely time with a sweet little girl. If only Sarah wouldn't point out no one expected Darcie to stick around longer than a few days.

Sam shuffled into the kitchen. He sniffed. "What's that smell?"

"Chocolate chip cookies." Darcie headed to the cabinet for glasses. "Why don't you get the milk and join us?"

The boy didn't hesitate. Fifteen minutes later, the three of them sat at the table, happily dipping their cookies in milk and smiling at each other over the rims of their glasses. Darcie couldn't remember the last time she'd felt so content and, dare she think it, happy?

She could even entertain the notion she wouldn't be found here, on top of this Ozark mountain. That a new life awaited her. One of freedom and honesty. As soon as she found that package of Tony's. Then things would be wonderful. No more hiding.

~

York stormed straight to his office and slammed the door. The thought of Darcie knowing his shame, the way his wife betrayed him, was like a knife to the gut. Made him less of a man. Weak. If he put such a spineless man in his novels, he'd lose his readers. People wanted a strong hero. One who took life by the horns, threw it to the ground, and hog-tied it.

He fell back into his chair. Lately, that's all he used it for. Its sole purpose was to catch him as he fell in a depressed slump. Certainly not for writing.

Dinner was meant to be a family affair. Time to reconnect with his children and possibly get to know Darcie better. See what made the woman tick. Why would someone so young and pretty be content as a baby-sitter in a small country town? Her presence shouldn't be a war zone between her and his ten-year-old son.

An aroma drifted up the stairs, pulling him from his thoughts. York lifted his nose and sniffed. Cookies? When was the last time someone other than Mrs. Olsen baked cookies?

He pushed from his chair and eased the door open. Sarah's giggle lifted his spirits, and he jogged down the stairs feeling lighter than when he'd climbed them. Despite the fog of sadness surrounding Darcie, things did look a little brighter around the house.

The picture of her smiling at his children greeted him as he entered the kitchen. Sarah's mouth sported a chocolate ring. "Cookies, Daddy! I helped make them."

"You did?" He tousled her hair and mouthed a thank you to Darcie, admiring the flush of pleasure that rose in her cheeks.

"Uh-huh. Aren't they good?"

York lifted one to his mouth and bit it in half. "Delicious."

His daughter beamed.

"We forgot to talk about days off." He transferred his attention to Darcie. "If you're in agreement, you'll have the weekends. I devote my weekdays to writing."

"Sure." She looked surprised. "But I can help with the kids all week. I've no where else to go."

"Shopping. Visiting friends. You'll still live here. Surely there are people you can reconnect with." How could he write an element of romance in his novels, yet not be able to string a complete sentence together with a real woman? An employee? Even Mrs. Olsen left him tongue-tied. When she wasn't nagging him about moving on with his life, that is.

Darcie rose and cleared the table. "That'll be fine. I'll make sure I'm out of your hair on the weekends."

Scarlet circles highlighted her cheeks. Her normally full lips drew into a stern line.

Where had he messed up this time? "That isn't what I meant." Why couldn't women be as easy to get along with as the heroines in his novels?

"Then what exactly did you mean?" She planted fists on slim hips and glared.

"Only that I don't want you to feel as if you owe us twenty-four, seven." He raised his eyes to the roof then marched outside. Women!

The moon cast the yard in silver. York perched on the porch railing and stared in the direction his old house used to stand. Nothing left there now but the foundation, and even that was fading. Mother Nature slowly claimed back what man took from her.

A door slammed overhead and a light switched on, sending a beam of gold through the night. York sighed. "Sam, Sarah, time for bed."

"We're already up here, Daddy." His daughter leaned over the banister. "Darcie asked us to go ahead and get ourselves ready. She said we're old enough."

York looked up. "You aren't too old for me to tuck in, are you?"

She grinned. "Never."

He took the stairs two-at-a-time while she ran squealing to her room. Sarah pounced on her bed and yanked the blankets over her head. York plopped beside her, tickling her through the covers. He glanced over to see Darcie scowling from the doorway.

"I thought someone was dying in here." She crossed her arms. "Didn't you think I'd do my job? You had to come and check up on me? Sam's ten and Sarah's eight. They don't need someone to dress them."

"Whoa!" York raised his hands. 'Is there something wrong with me saying goodnight? I wasn't checking up on you." He stood. "Somehow, I've offended you. I'm sorry. I thought maybe you needed time alone."

"Well, I don't." She whirled and stalked away.

York shook his head. He'd never get it right.

After tucking the blankets around Sarah, he stepped to her window to pull the curtains closed. A car slowed in front of the house, then sped off. Usually days went by without another driver on the road. If he wasn't mistaken, he'd seen that car before. Recently.

# CHAPTER SIX

"Good morning. You must be Darcie. My, aren't you a pretty thing." A bird of a woman with enough wrinkles to map out the country greeted Darcie when she stumbled down the stairs Wednesday morning. "I'm Mrs. Olsen. The maid, cook, housekeeper. Pick up whatever needs picking up. You name it. I'm a woman of all trades, so to speak." The woman's exuberance reminded Darcie of her grandmother, putting her immediately at ease.

"I'm sorry I haven't welcomed you properly. My brother's had a bit of tummy ache. An ulcer, I'm sure. York wants me to be here more now. Wouldn't be fitting to leave two young people alone, now would it? Good thing my brother is feeling better. It was quite a chore coming here late at night to chaperone." The woman flitted around the kitchen, keeping up a monologue the entire time. Darcie grew exhausted watching her. "There's fresh coffee. Let me fix you a cup. Have a seat right there. I've just mixed a batch of biscuits. Tell me about yourself. I want to know everything. We're going to be great friends."

The pounding of the kids' footsteps saved Darcie from having to answer. "Mrs. Olsen!" Sarah launched herself into the older woman's arms.

"Now, now. Sit down and have your breakfast." She plopped plates on the table, tossed biscuits on each, then ladled the thickest white gravy Darcie had ever seen over them. It would be a miracle if she didn't gain thirty pounds.

"Why didn't y'all eat the casseroles in the freezer?" Mrs. Olsen planted fists on her thin hips. "That's why I make them. Didn't anyone tell you that I have plenty of pre-cooked meals to get this family through the week?"

Darcie shook her head.

"Oh, well. What can you expect from a house with a man and children as the sole occupants? You're going to make such a difference, dear." She waved a hand. "Go on, eat."

She found the action difficult with the woman hovering. Darcie stuck a mouthful of biscuit into her mouth and almost fainted from pleasure. Her eyes popped open when York stepped into the room.

"Smells good." He kissed each of his children, patted Mrs. Olsen on the shoulder, and sat across the table from Darcie. He winked, and she almost choked. Who was this pleasant man and what had he done with her boss?

She wolfed her food like a ravenous animal then scooted back from the table. "Come on, guys. Time to get to school. Only a couple more days and you're free for the summer." She stared wide-eyed when they did as they were told without arguing.

Was Mrs. Olsen a miracle worker? Did her presence alone make a difference in the children's lives?

York wiped his mouth with a napkin. "I'd best be getting to work. See you two, ladies later."

Mrs. Olsen laughed. "The man's like two different people, sweetie. Depends on the kinds of dreams he has the night before. They're getting better, but, well, you know. Life's been rough."

"Okay." Darcie frowned then grabbed her purse and darted after the children. Doctor Jekyll and Mister Hyde. That's what the man was, and Mrs. Olsen was his all-knowing assistant.

Children dropped off on time, Darcie steered her massive car up and around the mountain. The shack that had been home to her during the first thirteen years of her life sat lopsided and sagging. "You look worse than you did fifteen years ago." She cut the engine and stared at the eye-sore. "Who would've thought I'd ever find myself back here." She'd vowed to never set foot on the scrape of a land parcel.

Before she could change her mind, Darcie strode toward the beaten front door. "It's no surprise no one's moved in here." Embarrassed to be talking to a weather beaten pile of wood, she glanced around the silent clearing. "I'm losing my mind. No doubt about it."

She kicked at a loose board then stepped over the fallen front stoop. "If I break a leg, I'll have no one to blame but myself. And Tony, for getting me in this mess. What would Mr. York Wardell say if he could see me now?" The door fell with a crash when she pushed on it. "Wonderful."

The horrors of her childhood assaulted her when she stepped across the threshold. The many men in her mother's life. The stench of stale cigarette smoke and beer. The wail of her baby brother. The many times Darcie had fled the house in terror when one of her "uncles" wanted special attention. Tears welled. She wiped a hand across her eyes with more force than necessary.

Temptation to turn and run overwhelmed her. Forget Tony's last words. She didn't have the strength to do this. Not yet. Despite her misgivings, she shuffled forward, kicking up years of dust.

A tattered, faded curtain hung in the frame of the one bedroom her mother had claimed to entertain her guests. Darcie couldn't force herself to move inside. She turned to the half-haphazardly boarded up back porch where she'd shivered more nights than she'd been warm. The same make-shift bedroom where her brother had died one winter from pneumonia. That had been the last night Darcie had slept beneath this roof.

A sigh rose from deep in her, only to be choked off by a sob. Grandma had saved her. Paramedics had removed the dead infant from Darcie's arms, and her grandmother moved the stricken teenage girl to her own humble two-bedroom house. She'd told Darcie God had intervened. Well, He hadn't moved in time to save Davie. She hadn't seen her mother since. Was she dead? Alive? Lying somewhere in a drunken stupor?

She sniffed and stepped to the window. Where could Tony have hidden it? There wasn't much here. An old well dug too shallow. The water used to taste of sulphur. A tilting building her mother had proudly called a barn, and this. This thing that could barely be called a house. Never a home.

Shoving aside the squeaky back door, she marched across the weed grown lawn toward the barn, hoping it wouldn't fall down upon her head. She shrieked when a coyote streaked out the door and past her legs, something furry hanging from its mouth. "Let's hope that's all that's living in here." Her words fell like ghost leaves in the dim recesses.

Rusty tools lay in forgotten stacks. Moldy bales of hay waited, never to be fed to hungry bovine. A mewing from the corner attracted her attention. Darcie followed the sound.

Six kittens scampered around discarded cords of wood. "Oh." She knelt beside them. "Was that your momma that beast had in its mouth?" She glanced around for signs of a larger cat. "Well, we can't leave you here or you'll be its next meal."

Darcie lifted a battered metal tub and chased the kittens until she'd captured every one. "Sam and Sarah will love you. Tony's quest will have to wait."

~

"She's hiding something, York. I can tell about these things." Mrs. Olsen plopped a meaty sandwich on his desk. "Mark my words, it ain't good."

"Oh?" The pastrami and cheese smelled wonderful. He hadn't realized the time until she'd brought his lunch. His stomach growled in response.

"She doesn't quite meet your eyes when you ask about her. Have you noticed?" Mrs. Olsen folded her arms and leaned against the desk. "The children seem taken with her, though. You know I ain't one to gossip. I never go around spreading untruths. You know that."

Yeah, he did. The dear woman could call it what she wanted, but her tongue wagged looser than an unhinged door.

"I remember her. Lived on the other side of the mountain with her no-good mother. Then Macille took her in. Do you remember? That girl lived a life no one should have had to endure. What do you think brought her back here?"

"A job." He bit into the sandwich and closed his eyes in bliss.

"It's more than that." Mrs. Olsen shook her head. "I aim to find out what. I love a good mystery. She's hurting, don't you think? One more reason why she wouldn't want to come back to a town that never treated her right."

"She had her reasons, I suspect."

"Uh-huh." She pushed away from the counter. "How's the writing? Over the slump?"

"Getting there."

"Does your muse have hair the color of a ripe strawberry and just a smattering of freckles?" She cackled and put a hand on his shoulder. "Don't let the past keep you from your future."

"What is that supposed to mean?"

"Don't push aside the chance to love again, is all I'm saying. Don't let Michelle's bad deeds sour you. God heals the deepest wounds." She laid her other hand on his left shoulder and kneaded. "You're a good man. You've got two beautiful children. Darcie's a pretty girl."

York shrugged her off and rose. "I'm not interested."

"Sure you aren't." Mrs. Olsen laughed and grabbed a dishtowel. "Famous last words, mister author man."

"You beat all, old woman." York laughed. "Now mind your own business." If he could find another woman with a heart like his housekeeper's, he'd snatch her up and never let go. Mr. Olsen had been a lucky man.

Darcie's reasons for returning to Shadow Springs would surface in time. York hoped her reasons wouldn't affect his family in a negative way.

He stepped outside to soak in some of the afternoon sun. His wanderings led him to the mailbox beside the road. He pulled open the door and reached inside. The envelope on top promised a royalty check. He smirked. If he didn't get to producing, these would come fewer and farther between.

A dark navy car drove slowly toward him and York marched to the middle of the road to flag them down. The driver's side window rolled down about three inches giving him a glimpse of dark hair on the driver and the shape of a passenger in the opposite seat.

"You lost?" He placed one hand on the door. "I noticed you driving by last night."

"Just looking for a friend who may have returned to these parts." The man's voice sounded as gravelly as if he smoked three packs a day of cheap cigarettes.

"You got a name for this friend?" The back of York's neck prickled.

"Not that I'm wanting to share. We're not even sure they're here. Now, unless you want to lose the toe of those fine cowboy boots, I suggest you step back from the car. Unless you got information of a newcomer around here."

"Other than you, you mean?"

York jumped back as the car sped away. He'd always trusted his instincts, whether they proved true or not. And right now they told him those men were up to no good.

# CHAPTER SEVEN

Darcie stashed the tub in the back seat of her car and headed down the mountain to pick up the children. She'd continue her search another time. Mewing serenaded her, and her heart felt lighter than it had in months. Since she had yet to see any signs of an animal on his land, York would most likely have a fit, but she'd find good homes for the kittens. After she enjoyed them a bit.

She pulled into the parent pick-up line at the school and thrust the car into park. She glanced back at the kittens, and giggled. Six balls of fur romped and climbed around the back seat. Good thing she'd had the sense of mind to bring her own car. Their little nails couldn't hurt these tattered seats. Her gaze lifted, and she froze.

Two men stood on the corner across the street, arms folded, staring in her direction. Were they staring at her, or someone else? Their dark suits looked out of place in the little town of Shadow Springs. Especially standing beside the parent pick-up at school. Her mouth filled with cotton.

Sam and Sarah emerged from the building and she frantically waved them over. "Come on. Hurry now. We don't want to be late for dinner. That would be rude to Mrs. Olsen."

"It's only three o'clock," Sam informed her, climbing in. His eyes widened at the sight of the kittens.

"Kittens!" Sarah squealed.

Once both children were inside, Darcie pressed the gas hard enough to bang the children against the backseat. "Sorry. Y'all put on your seatbelts."

"Dad's allergic to cats," Sam stated.

"Of course he is." Darcie stared out her rearview mirror.

Were they still there? Would the men follow? She gasped and hit the brake in order to avoid colliding with the vehicle in front of her. Her heart almost pounded through her ribcage.

*Relax. They're probably just fathers off work early and picking up their children. Yeah, and Santa Claus is real.* She swerved around the SUV in front of them and sped away from the school. Hopefully the children were occupied enough with the kittens not to notice her anxiety.

"You're speeding." Sam leaned over the front seat. "Dad's a stickler for the rules. If you get a ticket, he'll probably fire you."

Oh, he'd like that, wouldn't he, the little scamp. "And I said to put on your seatbelt. I don't think he'd be too excited about your lack of one. We wouldn't want to get into an accident and have you go through the front windshield." Her knuckles whitened on the steering wheel. Over-reaction had always been one of her major character flaws. She forced herself to relax, certain she created a dire situation where none existed.

"We'll definitely have an accident if you keep driving crazy."

"How was school today?" Darcie figured changing the subject would be safer than arguing with a ten-year-old about driving skills.

"Better now." Sarah held up a calico kitten high enough Darcie could see it through the window. "I want to keep this one. Do you think Dad will let me?"

"We'll see." Darcie kept scanning the road behind them. Her heart plummeted to the pit of her stomach.

A dark sedan pulled close enough she could make out two men in the front seat. Could she lose them?

They couldn't be looking for her. The woman they looked for didn't have children. While married to Tony, Darcie had gone through a blonde faze. She'd only recently gone back to her natural color.

She pressed the accelerator, then slowed. Darcie couldn't do this again. Images of Tony and herself lying bleeding beside the highway flashed through her mind. She'd been driving that night too. She couldn't risk the children. She'd grown up here. Surely she could find a back way home and lose them.

"Where are we going?" Sam asked.

"I thought we'd take the long way home. Get better acquainted."

"Why? You live with us. How much more acquainted do we need to get?" He quipped.

And Darcie thought Sam was warming to her.

"I just want to look around where I grew up. Get familiar with the area again. Relax. You're way too tense for a little boy." Darcie turned left, up the back side of the mountain, then a sharp right down a barely traveled dirt road. She stopped and watched behind them.

The sedan sped past. She smiled. Yep, a mountain out of a mole hill. "Okay, Sam, you win. Home it is."

"Are you hiding from someone?" His eyes widened. "Because you're acting just like a woman from one of those movies Dad doesn't like me to watch." He leaned against the front seat, arms hanging over the front.

She backed onto the road and turned toward home. "Why would you ask that?" *Oh, please don't tell your father you think I'm hiding from someone. I've nowhere to go until I find Tony's package.*

"You're acting strange, and your clothes are dirty." Sam raised his eyebrows. "I bet you're a killer, or a bank robber, and you only took this job to hide out."

"You ought to write your own books. You obviously have your father's imagination." Darcie glanced down. Mud streaked one leg of her jeans and dirt marked the tee-shirt she wore. "I went for a hike. If I hadn't, you wouldn't have a lap full of cat right now." Would the lies ever end? "I told you to put on your seat belt!"

"Something funny's going on here." Sam folded his arms and plopped back against the seat.

"No, nothing funny." At least that part was true. She pulled her gaze from the rearview mirror and concentrated back on the road. She tried desperately to remember everything Tony had told her before he died. A package. A shack. Her mother's place? Or had he meant her grandmother's?

And something about a list of important names. Darcie pounded the steering wheel. What was it?

He'd made her promise. Said finding the information would protect her. Protect her from what? And why did she need protecting? She knew Tony's gambling had gotten out of control. The fact she didn't have a nickel to her name was testimony to that wonderful piece of news. But he'd made her promise to run. To hide. To find…something. There had to be more to it. She needed to carve out the time to find out what he'd hidden.

~

When Darcie and the kids climbed out of the car, disheveled, dirty, late, and clutching kittens, York clenched his jaw tight enough to cause a spasm in his cheek. What had the woman done now?

"Where did you get those?" He forced the words between his lips.

Mrs. Olsen laughed, clapped him on the shoulder, then disappeared into the house.

"Aren't they cute, Daddy?" Sarah shoved one at him. "I'm keeping this one. Can I?"

"I found them," Darcie explained. "I couldn't just leave the little darlings." She lowered her voice.

"Their mother was eaten by a coyote."

"They stay in the shed." York shook his head and turned to go back in the house. His nose and throat already itched, and he hadn't touched the things. "And I want them all gone before the end of the week."

"Daddy!"

He glanced over his shoulder. Sarah's dark eyes filled with tears. Darcie's odd golden ones watched him over his daughter's head. "Okay," he nodded. "Except that one. But it stays outside."

"Softie." Mrs. Olsen wiped her hands on a dish towel as he entered the house. "Who is it you can't refuse? Your daughter or her nanny?"

"That's enough." York marched past her. "Is it time for dinner or not?"

She chuckled. "Dinner is served, your majesty. Oh, king of the castle, I live to do your bidding." She turned and led the way. "But you might want to tell that sprite out there to clean up first."

He stopped and waited until the others came inside. "Dinner is ready. Darcie you need to clean up. Kids, wash your face and hands."

"Yes, Sir!" Darcie clicked her heels and saluted. "Anything you say, Sir!" She spun and marched with exaggerated steps from the room. If not for the high spots of color on her cheeks, York would've thought she goofed around.

He drummed his fingers on the table as he waited, his gaze following Mrs. Olsen around the room. "I apologize. I know you like to get to your room in time for your shows. From now on, the days you work, just leave the food. Obviously, early dinner nights are a thing of the past."

"Darcie is perfectly capable of finishing up the meals once I get them started. Never could figure out why you like eating so early anyway. Most people eat at five or later." She sat a bowl of biscuits in front of him. "And there's enough casseroles in the freezer to feed y'all for a week."

"Because most days I forget to eat lunch." He sounded like a pouting child, even to his ears. An early dinner left time for ice cream later. A habit he'd enjoyed since childhood. What was wrong with him? Did it bother him to see his children having fun with a woman other than their mother? When was the last time they'd had fun with him?

The others barged in and Mrs. Olsen excused herself to go to her room. York watched as his children bowed their heads to bless the food. He raised an eyebrow at Darcie until she followed their example.

His gaze flicked to her face as the children rambled about their day. She wore a haunted look and cast repeated glances toward the window.

"And Darcie was speeding." Sam shoveled in another forkful of casserole, talking around the noodles. "She acted like she was running away from someone."

"Sam wouldn't put on his seatbelt." Darcie's fork clattered to the side of her plate. She stared earnestly at York. "I would never jeopardize the children."

He sighed. "Sam, stop tormenting Mrs. Thayer. The two of you need to learn to get along." He frowned at his son. "I'd better not hear of you refusing to wear a seatbelt again, young man."

"You're taking her side?"

"I'm not taking anyone's side." He tossed his napkin on the table. The words of Mrs. Olsen haunted him. Was Darcie running? What secret did she hide behind those cat eyes?

# CHAPTER EIGHT

The last day of school, and the kids acted like they were hyped-up on a pound of sugar. By the time Darcie dropped them off at school, she wanted nothing more than to go back to bed. Instead, she sat in front of the local supermarket with a cardboard box of furry kittens, minus one calico. She lifted her hair off her neck and allowed the cool breeze to dry her sweat.

To top it all off, York expected her to attend a make-shift football game and go camping. She hated both. Plus, the temperature today peaked at 89 degrees with an unnecessary amount of humidity. She forced a smile to her face when a mother and her young girl approached.

"How much for a kitten?" The woman laid a hand against her daughter's back.

"Free to a good home."

The little girl squealed and grabbed a grey fluff of fur then squashed the meowing kitten to her chest. For a moment Darcie feared for the feline's neck, but the girl's mother relaxed her daughter's hold and gave her a word of caution.

Within the hour, Darcie tossed an empty box into the closest dumpster and drove back up the mountain. She'd seen no sign of the dark sedan with the mystery men inside since leaving the school yesterday, but couldn't resist several glances in her rearview mirror anyway.

Back home, she fed the calico kitten then stepped into the air-conditioned kitchen. She still found the term 'home' uncomfortable since the massive log structure belonged to the Wardell family and not her, but for lack of any other place to lay her head, she considered the place her home as well. At least for now.

She snuck to the foot of the stairs and listened for the sound of York working. Silence greeted her ears. That meant the door was shut, and he wasn't to be disturbed short of a catastrophe. Long, solitary hours loomed ahead of her.

The ever-present search for the "package" called. She shoved the urge aside.

The rising temperature outside, combined with her foul mood, made her want to find anything to do besides dig around in ramshackle, dusty, places.

She discovered a notebook in a drawer and sat at the kitchen table. Time to make some notes. Tony's words rang in her mind. "It's hidden in the shack used for…" Then nothing. Her mother's house didn't look used for anything.

As far as she knew, the same went for her grandmother's. Besides providing a home for stray cats, the barn also yielded no information. But they'd been used once. What for? If she could think of their prior use, maybe she could figure out which one Tony spoke about.

She folded her arms and let her head fall forward. If her grandmother were still alive, she'd tell Darcie to call on God for help. Darcie shrugged. Right. Like He helped her all the times she'd called on Him before.

"What am I missing?" She tossed the ink pen on the blank notebook.

"Talking to yourself?" York strolled to a cupboard and withdrew a glass.

"Maybe."

He withdrew a pitcher from the refrigerator and filled his glass with lemonade. "Something bothering you?"

"Nope. I'm just peachy. A bit bored is all." Why was he so interested all of a sudden? Darcie crossed her arms.

He leaned against the counter. "What are you writing?"

"Grocery list."

He raised his drink for a sip. "Really? It's blank. We must not need anything. Besides, Mrs. Olsen usually does the shopping."

"Aren't you supposed to be working?"

"Touchy, touchy. I'll go with you to pick up the kids. I'll need to be at the field shortly after that to get the team suited up. The game on the last day of school is always a lot of fun. No pads or gear, just flags." He drained his drink and left the room. "I'll leave you to your secrets."

*That is one strange man.* Handsome, but very weird. She'd have to be more careful regarding her hunt. His eyes had held a suspicious glint. She couldn't afford to be fired. What she did on her own time was her business.

Three hours later, she climbed into the passenger side of his truck dressed in denim walking shorts and a tee-shirt. Camping equipment filled the bed. She might as well resign herself to twenty-four hours of torture. He'd better not ask her to skin the fish. If she didn't need the job so badly, she'd have refused to accompany them and told her boss to jump in the lake.

Sam and Sarah chattered non-stop about the one-night camping trip. Sam about catching a fish larger than his father would, and Sarah about sharing a tent with Darcie. The little girl's excitement raised Darcie's spirits. Maybe the two of them could squeeze in a short hike while the boys pursued their competition.

Once they reached the ball field, Sarah grabbed Darcie's hand and tugged her toward the bleachers. Sam proudly stated he was the team water boy and dashed off after his father.

Sarah chose the highest bleacher. Darcie settled back against the chain link backrest. Within the next twenty minutes, the home side of the stands filled. She smiled, remembering the excitement of a football game in a small town. Even if it was only a practice game. A chance for the players to burn off steam and celebrate the end of another school year.

The crowd roared as the team burst onto the field, followed by their coach. York wore coaching shorts and a tee-shirt with the team's name emblazoned across the back. Shadow Spring's Cougars. The title of coach seemed to fit the strapping man better than author. Darcie settled back and allowed herself the pleasure of watching him stalk the sidelines.

"It's great to see you here." Mrs. Olsen plopped beside her. "I never miss a game. Even one just for fun. Isn't York handsome?"

"Very." Realizing what she'd said, Darcie clamped a hand over her mouth.

"Yuck." Sarah leaned forward. "Grownups are gross."

Darcie returned Mrs. Olsen's smile and removed her hand. "I'm not fond of football, but the scenery is definitely better than I remember. It's got to be better than the camping trip York has planned for tonight."

The older woman laughed and pulled cold bottles of water from a tote she set at her feet. She offered one to Darcie and Sarah, then leaned against the fence. "I like football because you can watch and talk at the same time. York has done a great job volunteering with the team until a replacement is hired. He'll miss the boys." She eyed Darcie sternly. "He mentioned a night at the river. Said it would be a great chance to reconnect with Sam. I'm wondering why he's having you and Sarah tag along. Seems to me he's wanting to get closer to you too." She wiggled her eyebrows. "I'm not much for camping, but guess I can chaperone for one night."

Butterflies danced the tango in Darcie's stomach.

"You don't want to hear the plays?"

"I don't understand the fundamentals, dear." Mrs. Olsen waved a hand in dismissal. "York is like a son to me. I never had any children of my own. Needless to say, I'm very protective of the man. What brings you back to Shadow Springs?"

"A job?"

"That's what York said. Forgive me if I think there's more to things than that." She dug in her purse and pulled out a few dollars. "Sarah, why don't you run to the concession stand and buy some nachos?"

Darcie wanted to keep the girl beside her to fend off the forthcoming uncomfortable questions. She stalled by guzzling from her water bottle when Sarah left.

"Well?" Mrs. Olsen peered at her over the rim of her spectacles. "Why would someone with such a tragic childhood want to come back?"

"To lay old ghosts to rest?"

"Are you telling me or asking?" Mrs. Olsen placed a hand on Darcie's knee. "Sweetie, you strike me as a good girl. But you carry a secret, not to mention the nervous habit you have of placing a hand on your stomach."

Darcie choked and sputtered, spraying water on the seat in front of them and an older couple sitting there. They turned and glared.

"Sorry." Darcie wiped her mouth on her sleeve and took a deep breath. "I lost my husband and unborn child in a car accident. I had no where else to go but back here."

"And you want this old woman to mind her own

business."

"It's painful to talk about."

"Okay. Your news is safe with me. Life goes on, dear. Time heals wounds, and what's left, God can handle." Mrs. Olsen's lips slipped into a soft smile. "But I think you're struggling with that, too, am I right?"

Darcie nodded. Thankfully, the other woman appeared satisfied with Darcie's answer. It wasn't like she lied. Not exactly. She'd withheld information. Facts Mrs. Olsen didn't need to know.

During half-time, Suzy Bouchee breezed onto the sidelines wearing a larger version of the cheerleaders' costumes. Mrs. Olsen tsked-tsked.

Suzy waved her arms over her head, clapped off a beat, and bounced off the field as twelve screaming girls leaped on. Darcie giggled. Almost thirty years old and the woman fancied herself a cheerleader. She'd been head of the squad during high school. Obviously, Suzy relived her glory days as cheerleading coach.

"It is a bit ridiculous," Mrs. Olsen explained. "But no one else wanted to do it after the last woman quit. Couldn't deal with the drama. My guess is Suzy's taking over has more to do with York than cheerleading. And that skirt! At her age. It's shameful. Thankfully, York sees right through her ploys."

Relief welled in Darcie as warming as the setting sun. Hopefully, the man liked his women more down-to-earth and wholesome. She could be that. Once she kept Tony to his deceitful promise, that is. Did she want to see whether something could develop with York?

Rather than watch the girls jump up and down to scratchy boom-box music, she scanned the surrounding crowd. Sarah climbed the bleacher steps, carefully balancing a tray of nachos covered with cheese. A couple of teenage boys strutted in front of a group of giggling girls. Someone screamed, then laughed.

Darcie glanced beneath the spectator stands for the source of the noise. Her search ended as she looked directly under her and made out two pairs of legs in dark trousers and dress shoes. At a football game?

Could it be the two men who'd followed them from school?

"You take one, I'll take the other." The man's voice pierced through the lull in spectator screams. "There's only two women newly arrived in town. It's got to be one of them."

Heart beating with the speed of a jet, Darcie turned back to the game. Her mouth dried, and she swallowed against the lump in her throat. When she peered again under the bleachers, the men were gone.

# CHAPTER NINE

The Cougars emerged victorious from the scrimmage game and spirits were high in York's truck. Except for Darcie's. The sight of the overly dressed feet and legs of the two strangers cast a pall over a trip she hadn't been excited on taking in the first place. She couldn't search while surrounded by Wardells and she had to continuously field Mrs. Olsen's probing questions. The secrets Darcie carried weighed more with each passing day.

York headed out of town to the river ten miles outside city limits. Darcie smiled, remembering the times she and Tony had 'sparked' on the riverbank. The thick foliage provided coverage for many courting teenagers.

Sneaking a look at York's profile, she wondered how many starry-eyed girls he'd taken into the bushes. Being the head jock during his senior year, she guessed plenty. What should she care? York

Wardell was her over-bearing, monologue-talking employer. One who *requested* she accompany his family on a camping trip. She crossed her arms and stared out the window.

By the time they pulled into a vacant spot, complete with cleared area for a tent and sporting a concrete picnic table, she felt a full-blown pout fest coming on. She shoved open her door and grabbed the first thing her hand touched out of the truck's bed.

Great. The cooking stove. Well, she wouldn't be doing the cooking. She'd done plenty during the many times their electricity had been shut off when she was growing up. Mrs. Olsen could have the pleasure.

"Relax." York reached across her for one of the tents. "It's only for one night."

How did he know she was upset about spending the night with nature?

"That look on your face would scare away a grizzly." He laughed and plopped the tent in the center of the cleared area.

Darcie spun. Were there bears here? She eyed the thicket of trees. Didn't they stay farther up the mountain? She couldn't remember the last time one had wandered into town.

"He's teasing." Sam lugged the other tent beside the first. York winked at her over his son's head.

Teasing? Mister cool and collected? Darcie's face heated and she suspected an alternative motive for being invited along. Was it possible York liked her? Or did he want to make her feel more at home?

Not sure how to feel about that possibility, she

set to work with a vengeance emptying the back of the truck.

Her bad mood needed to dissipate, and soon. She had no proof the two strangers had been talking about her. Hadn't she let fear rule her for long enough?

Camp in order, York and Sam headed to the river, fishing poles clutched in their fists. Mrs. Olsen pulled up a folding chair and opened a book then waved for Darcie and Sarah to go "find something fun to do". Darcie took Sarah's hand and led her down a well-worn path for a hike. Anything beat sitting around staring at a fire pit with no flames. And fishing…no way. That had to be the most boring sport in the world.

"Dad, said we could make S'mores tonight. Yum." Sarah's chatter filled the air around them. "It's been a long time since we've done anything fun. Not since Mommy died."

How sad. Had York shoved aside his children for mourning? Darcie hoped he didn't have plans on replacing his wife with her. If a relationship developed between the two of them, she wanted it to be on her own merits. Not based on a dead woman. She squeezed Sarah's hand. "Let's see if we can find some wildflowers."

"Okay!" Sarah skipped down the path ahead of her. "Look huckleberries!"

Darcie stooped and plucked a Black-eyed Susan. It's dark button center was a beautiful contrast to the bright yellow petals. Downy Phlox dotted the foliage along the trail with shots of pink.

To their right, the man-made lake sparkled in the

late-afternoon sun. The mountain provided a majestic backdrop. Darcie couldn't help but appreciate the splendor of the view. She paused and stared across the water. She could make out the form of York and Sam casting lines into the water. Ripples spread across the lake's surface.

A branch snapped behind her. She whirled. "Sarah?"

"Yeah?" The little girl rose from behind a bush.

"Come back where I can see you." Darcie stared into the foliage behind her.

Were the shadows deeper in there? She held out her hand for Sarah. "Let's head back to camp."

Leaves rustled and she ran, dragging the little girl behind her. Once they reached the relative safety of the tent, Darcie laughed. The lurker was most likely an animal more afraid of her than she was of it.

"Why'd we run?" The flowers in Sarah's hand sagged, begging for drink.

"I thought it would be fun." Darcie dug a plastic cup from a nearby bag. "Let's put some water in here before those flowers die." They made their way to the lake's edge.

York waved and Sam held up a stringer with two fish. Wonderful. They'd be having bass for dinner.

"They caught something!" Flowers forgotten, Sarah dashed to her father's side.

Darcie cast another glance down the trail they'd walked. Although she tried to convince herself the movement in the bushes was an animal, she couldn't shake the feeling that someone had watched them.

~

York stirred the embers of the fire and glanced at Darcie's highlighted face. "You seem to be surviving all right. Is this your first time camping?"

"I camped most of my childhood right under my own roof." Darcie stared into the dancing flames. "That's what happens when your water and electricity get shut off on a regular basis. I cooked more dinners on a Coleman stove than a forest ranger. And that saying about a bear going, you know, in the woods, well, I could beat that."

His laugh rang, startling roosting birds from the trees. "This is different. This is fun."

"Depends on your definition of fun, I guess." She picked up a stick and poked at a smoldering log. So much entertainment, Mrs. Olsen had already retired to the tent.

"What is your idea of fun?"

"Curling up with a good book. Watching a movie with someone I love. A good dinner."

"I can help with two of those. The fish will be finished in just a minute and there's a book in my backpack. A bestseller."

Darcie pulled the bag to her and reached inside. "The Bible?"

He laughed again, enjoying the range of emotions across her pretty face. Anger and disbelief. Her odd-colored eyes flashed. When was the last time he'd felt this carefree? "Have you read it?"

"No." She shoved it back. "And I don't intend to anytime soon."

They'd see about that. York vowed to get the woman to crack the pages before the month was out. He called Sam and Sarah out of the tent and divided fish and beans between four plates.

Despite Darcie's sour attitude, he enjoyed himself. The time to reconnect with his children was priceless. Getting to know what made Darcie tick came a close second.

Less than a week had passed, and he found himself drawn to the woman. He shook his head. He never would have guessed. Not after Michelle's betrayal. Darcie's animosity toward God bothered him, but he felt a drawing toward the Creator lurking beneath her smattering of freckles. Waiting. In the meantime, he'd work on erasing the haunted look in her eyes.

After dinner, the children raced to get the makings of S'mores. Within minutes both children had marshmallows crammed on straightened wire hangers and suspended over the fire's flames.

York smiled at their antics. Sarah's caught on fire and she waved the hanger viciously back and forth. "Don't, Sarah. Blow on it."

The sticky goo dislodged and smattered against Darcie's bare leg. She yelped and leaped to her feet, swiping at the burning mess on her calf. "Get it off!" She jumped up and down, scattering dishes. Then promptly fell to her backside over the chair she'd sat on.

"Be still!" York raced to her side and plucked the marshmallow from her leg. "Sit down and let me take a look. Sam, get the first aid kit."

"I'm sorry." Sarah squatted next to them, her eyes brimming with tears. "I wanted to put the fire out."

"It's okay." Darcie pulled her close. "I'll be fine."

York knelt in front of Darcie and placed her foot in his lap. A raw patch of skin greeted him. It had to hurt. The rising emotion as he ran his hand down her leg, took his breath away. She'd shaved recently, her skin like silk beneath his hand.

Raising his head, their gazes locked. His hand stilled as his heart raced. An overwhelming urge to kiss her wound came over him. Sam's arrival broke the spell, and he lowered his head.

*Lord, what am I doing? I can't be attracted to a woman who doesn't know You. Maybe she does. But she doesn't care for what she knows. That's alien to me.* York smoothed antibiotic cream on the burn. His heart clenched at Darcie's sharp intake of breath. He smoothed on a large band-aid then stood. "It's not too bad. You should be all right." York busied himself cleaning up the strewn paper plates and cups.

Darcie murmured behind him, calming the still sobbing Sarah. She might not care for God, but Darcie obviously felt affection for York's children.

For the past six months, Mrs. Olsen had been after him to find a mother for them. Not a temporary solution such as a nanny. Could Darcie's fondness for Sam and Sarah, and York's disturbing but growing feelings for her be enough to make them a family?

# CHAPTER TEN

Giggles and shrieks of glee woke York the next morning. He pulled the pillow over his head to shut out the Sunday morning sun. Why wouldn't his kids ever sleep in? Then he remembered Darcie. She'd been there a week and had firmly attached herself in Sam's and Sarah's lives.

If he wasn't careful, she'd seem like a permanent fixture in his too. He needed to be sure he wanted that to happen, and if not, put a stop to it. Despite the allure of curly red hair and jade green eyes. The dimples and freckles didn't hurt either.

He glanced at his watch. Seven o'clock the second morning of summer break. He groaned and climbed from bed. Past experience taught him that once awake, he was up for the day. He lumbered to the window and parted the curtains.

Sarah had the kitten dressed in doll clothes and scampering across the yard. York smiled at the domestic picture. Darcie sat on a lawn chair, mug in hand, and laughed at his daughter's antics. Sam shook his head at the silliness of it all. Obviously ten was too old to indulge in such shenanigans.

The scene brightened and saddened York at the same time. He let the curtains fall into place. It should've been Michelle enjoying the children. Not a stranger who didn't seem much more than a child herself sometimes. Other times, she seemed older than Mrs. Olsen.

Pulling a tee-shirt over the cotton shorts he'd slept in, York made his way to the kitchen and the still hot pot of coffee. Relief at not having to make the brew himself welled in his chest. Mrs. Olsen knew his routine as well as her own.

A glance out the sliding door showed Darcie still sitting but staring toward the front of the house. Her smile had vanished. Her hand covered her stomach. York frowned. He'd get to the bottom of her secret before the weekend was over.

He opened the door and stepped onto the porch. Out of sight a car engine rumbled.

"Come on, Sarah." Darcie bolted to her feet and scooped the kitten in her arms. "Time for breakfast."

"I'm not hungry. I want to play with my baby."

"Sarah, now." Darcie cast a stern look at the girl and marched toward the house.

"Y'all mind Darcie, Sarah. Sam, you too." York frowned as Darcie moved into the house. "Cat stays outside," he reminded her. His throat and ears itched in anticipation of sharing a room with the feline.

She cast another glance toward the road. "I forgot. Sorry."

The wriggling mass of fur in her arms meowed as she backed off the porch and headed for the barn. After another of her glances toward the road, York stepped into the grass and marched around the corner. The road was empty.

~

Darcie thought she'd choke on her fear. When the dark sedan slowed in front of the house, she'd spilled her coffee and covered the movement by scooping up the kitten. They'd found her. She'd have to leave. Somehow, she'd have to find the strength to leave Sarah and Sam. And yes, York too. Why couldn't she have a normal life? With a family? Why'd she get sucked so soon into caring for a dark-haired family with eyes the color of chocolate?

With her hip, she pushed open the door to the barn and deposited the mewling kitten inside. Later, she'd come out and free it from the baby clothes Sarah had dressed it in. When she knew it was safe.

A scrap of paper flapped in the corner of the barn, drawing her attention. With trembling fingers she reached for the square of white embedded on a rusty nail and pulled it free. Her voice went hoarse as she whispered, "Give us what your husband hid, or meet his fate."

She crushed the threat in her fist and raised her other hand to cover the sound of her gasp. Tony promised the package he'd hidden would make her life better. Not fill it with threats. He'd been as deceitful in death as he'd been in life. Full of empty promises.

She fell onto an empty barrel and read the message again. How did they find her? She knew with high certainty the suited men at the school and the football game were the ones following her. Coincidences didn't happen in her life. Who had Tony gotten mixed up with? Had he told them where she once lived? Why would he?

Being stalked by a stranger made her limbs want to freeze with panic. Her skin crawled.

Taking a deep breath, she squared her shoulders, stuffed the warning into the pocket of her jeans, then marched to the house. She couldn't help but send anxious glances toward the road and the woods beyond. She had to focus more of her efforts on finding what Tony had hidden. If she did, and she handed it over, whatever *it* was, then maybe she could get on with her life. Maybe she could keep this new one.

It wouldn't be hard to imagine herself married to York and be the mother of Sam and Sarah. She already felt a strong attraction for the man and loved the children. Love for the father wouldn't be difficult.

The physical attraction was there. He made a good living and could provide well for her. It was definitely something to consider once the threat of danger was past. She sighed. The plans made her sound so heartless. When had she given up on finding good in life?

She brushed a hand across her stomach. She'd have a life to replace the one she'd lost.

Her steps faltered when York strolled around the

corner of the house. He shot her a puzzled look.

"You and I," his finger motioned from her to him. "Need to have a talk soon. When the children aren't around."

Her heart skipped a beat as he marched up the wooden steps and into the house. She almost called on her grandmother's God to save her. To make York forget his promise to talk. She shrugged. God had never been there for her before. Why should He start now?

York stood at the kitchen counter unloading bowls from the dishwasher.

"I'll make pancakes." Darcie brushed past him. "The kids don't need cereal every morning of the week."

"It's your day off and not your job." He lined four bowls on the counter and reached for a box of corn flakes. "I've already sent Mrs. Olsen into town."

"Fine. I'm making pancakes for myself and," She dumped mix into a bowl. "Oops, I've poured too much." She grabbed milk and added it to the dry mix in front of her. "Definitely can't put it back now." She turned and raised her eyebrows at him.

The corner of his mouth twitched. "You're a sassy thing, you know that?" He leaned closer to her ear. "But don't think your charm can dissuade me from finding out your secret." He straightened and went to sit at the kitchen table.

Her stomach clenched. He'd fire her for sure when he found out. Probably for the best.

In her quest to make a life for herself, she might be endangering his family. She'd grown too attached in such a short time. Something she swore wouldn't happen.

The children barged into the kitchen and, with the silence of stampeding buffalo, took their seats. As she prepared breakfast, despite the continuous chatter of the children, she felt York's gaze on her.

She needed to find that package before he forced her into a revealing conversation. She had the weekends off. She would use the excuse of shopping to leave the house then search her mother's land more thoroughly. After that, she'd move on to her grandmother's, not coming home until she'd found what Tony had hidden.

What if he'd hidden money? She slowed in her stirring of the batter. She could leave the country. Completely start fresh. Maybe in Europe. Her breath hitched.

Darcie prepared and ate breakfast in record time, then piled the dishes in the sink. "I'll clean these later. There's something I need to do today." She darted up the stairs to her room, faltering once when York called her name.

She grabbed her purse from the nightstand drawer and dashed back down the stairs.

"We'll talk when you get back," York called.

# CHAPTER ELEVEN

"We'll talk when you get back," Darcie mimicked. Not if she could help it. She liked where she was. She liked being nanny to Sam and Sarah. And no matter how much she tried to deny it, she felt a similar liking for York. More than liked him, if she was truthful. If only Tony hadn't left that stupid package hanging over her head.

She yanked the Impala's door open, climbed behind the wheel, shoved the key into the ignition then spun gravel out of the driveway and down the mountain. She drove cautiously around hair-pin mountain curves until she once again stared through the car's window at her mother's rundown shack.

"I might as well exhaust all possibilities of it being hidden here before I head to the other side of this mountain and search Grandma's place." Darcie slid from the car and slammed the door. The sound echoed, startling birds from the trees. "All Tony managed to say was shack. That could be half the old homes on this mountain." She kicked a rock and cringed at the sharp pain in her toe.

Her gaze ran over the house and sagging barn. As much as she dreaded it, she'd have to start pulling up boards and search under the floor. She marched to the trunk of the Chevy and retrieved the crow bar. She should've thought to bring a bigger variety of tools. She sighed and headed for the house.

The rickety porch squeaked beneath her weight. Watching each placement of her feet, she made her way inside and laughed as she stepped over the door she knocked down on her previous visit. No one to do the repairs now, was there?

The impact of the crow bar striking the wood floor vibrated against her arm. She cried out. She let the tool hang from an aching arm, then realized it would be easier to pull the boards up, rather than striking through them. Dummy.

Two hours later, with half of the living room floor torn up, she still hadn't found anything other than mice and a headache. She plopped to the dusty floor and laid her head on bent knees. Think, Darcie. Would Tony have had time to rip up a floor? Or pull down a wall?

She shook her head. He'd have stuffed the package in a place easily accessible, yet hidden. If she'd stopped to think before running full tilt ahead, she might have saved herself hard labor. She ran scared and knew it.

The thought of praying to the God she'd turned from rose to mind, and she pushed it aside. Maybe she should come clean to York and enlist his help. Maybe the man wouldn't turn her out. Yeah, right, and maybe purple oranges grew on trees.

She shoved to her feet and marched outside. Her gaze roamed the weed covered yard. Her childhood sanctuary. The tree house. She sprinted into the woods.

Tilted and weather beaten, the tree house perched between the branches of an ancient oak. Darcie smiled, remembering the many times she'd retreated here with a cherished library book. Had she mentioned the place to Tony?

She grasped the fraying rope and pulled herself up the trunk. Hand-over-hand and foot-over-foot. Her arms ached with the strain. It had seemed so much easier as a child. The rope slid through her hands, slicing into her palms. She hissed against the pain and glanced down. The ground seemed a hundred yards away. The rope slipped again.

It'd be quicker to finish the journey up than head down. She increased her speed, keeping her gaze on the rope rubbing against the floor of the tree house floor. *Please hold.* Only a few more inches.

The rope snapped. She stretched and grabbed the planks above her head. Her hopes plummeted to the ground along with the shredded fibers. It lay coiled beneath her like a snake ready to strike. With a grunt, she swung her leg up and over, pulling herself to safety.

Darcie lay with her cheek pressed against the rotting wood. Once she caught her breath, she rolled to her back. Nothing. The walls had more holes than they did wood. The floor beneath her was barely large enough to provide her a place to stretch out. She wouldn't need to search to realize climbing up here had been a futile waste of time. Not to mention she'd almost been injured.

She flopped back to her stomach and peered over the edge. There wouldn't be any jumping down. She studied the branches around her. Although thick and sturdy, they were too high off the ground for her to climb to safety. She was an idiot. And now she was stuck in a tree with no way down. All she needed was for the bad guys to show up.

Thunder rumbled in the distance.

~

With one ear tuned to his children's sibling rivalry from the direction of their rooms, York tried in vain to concentrate on the words staring at him from his computer screen. Darcie had been gone for hours and now the weather threatened with another summer storm. The weather channel issued a tornado watch.

*Relax, man. She grew up here. She'd know what to do if the weather turned bad.*

The sound of tires on gravel reached him through the open window. He rolled his chair to peer out, and grimaced at the sight of Suzy behind the wheel of her red convertible. He wished Mrs. Olsen was here to head the woman off. He sighed and rose. No help for it. He'd have to greet her.

"York!" Suzy called before she'd shut her car door. "I hope you're free next weekend. I'm having a Sunday barbecue, and I'd love for you to be my guest."

"The children and I will be attending church,

Suzy." He stepped onto the porch.

She waved him off. "The get together isn't until three. You've plenty of time. Have your nanny," she giggled. "Watch the children, and you can enjoy some time with your friends." She practically skipped to stand at the bottom of the steps and smiled up at him.

Why couldn't he find the woman attractive? Many men seemed drawn to the platinum hair and flawless complexion. Darcie's strawberry curls and hazel eyes swam before him. Where could she be?

"Darcie has the weekends off, Suzy. If I do choose to come, I'll be bringing Sam and Sarah."

"Oh well. If it can't be helped." She stepped up beside him. "I'll make sure there are other children there. That way, you won't have to spend every minute with them."

"They are *my* children."

A dark sedan cruised past, slowing. York watched with narrowed eyes until they moved on.

"Don't be a grump." Suzy placed a manicured paw on his arm. "Aren't you going to invite me in?"

"I'm sorry. But the kids and I were just leaving. Sam! Sarah!"

The thundering of their feet pounding down the stairs had never sounded so wonderful. He grinned as they slammed through the screen door.

Suzy frowned and took a step back. With obvious effort, she regained her composure. "I hope to see y'all next Sunday. It won't be the same if you aren't there."

York nodded. "We'll try." He turned and glanced at Sam's and Sarah's feet. "You two get shoes on.

We're going for a drive."

"Okay." They yelled in unison and barged back into the house. Within minutes they reappeared, feet slipped into flip-flops.

Suzy spun gravel backing from the drive and roared down the road.

"Where we going?" Sarah climbed behind the front seat, settling into the cab of the truck.

"To find Darcie." Fat rain drops splattered against the windshield before York turned the truck around. He laughed at the thought of Suzy's convertible. Had she gotten the top up in time?

"I thought today was her day off." Sam hooked his seatbelt across him.

"It is. I just wanted to get away."

"From Ms. Boushee?"

When had his son gotten so astute? York laughed. "Something like that. How about some ice cream?"

"Yippee!"

York scanned the sides of the road as he headed down the mountain, certain Darcie's car would be parked, broken down again, somewhere along the way. When they reached town with no sign of her, he felt the first prickles of worry. He had no reason to feel the way he did, but something told him she was in trouble.

He drove around town before pulling into the local drive-in burger joint. His mind stretched, trying to remember whether Darcie had family still living in Shadow Springs. She hadn't mentioned friends.

Would she have left, taking none of her

belongings with her? Had she had enough of being a nanny? He shook his head. Sam and Sarah seemed to like her, and she would have said something if she were leaving for good.

He ordered milk shakes for the three of them. His tasted like blended cardboard. The rain poured heavier now and lightening split the sky. "How about we eat this while we drive?"

The kids shrugged, clearly not caring what he chose to do since they had their lips pursed around straws. York drove back up the mountain and past his house, forcing his memory to recall where Darcie's childhood home had been.

He slowed around a sharp turn.

A gunshot echoed.

# CHAPTER TWELVE

"**D**ad?" Sam pulled away from his shake. "That sounded like a gun."

"Just the storm, Sam." York peered through the furiously wiping windshield wipers. It *had* sounded like a gunshot. Close too.

"I don't think so."

"It's thunder."

A sedan barreled around the corner, trees squealing.

York yanked the steering wheel and forced the truck against the face of the mountain. Mud and rocks sprayed behind them. Tree branches scratched along the side of the truck like prisoners reaching through the bars of their cells. He glanced up and followed the car's retreat through the rearview window, trying to catch a glimpse of the license plate. Fools. Everyone knows you don't take mountain roads fast. Not if you want to reach the bottom alive.

Tail lights glowed red. The sedan stopped and spun until it faced the way it had come. The car roared past again, slinging water.

Sarah screamed, Sam yelped, and York fought against the desire to barrel after the other vehicle and confront the driver for his recklessness.

Instead, he slammed on the brakes as he rounded the next bend.

A man lay in the road. A river of scarlet flowed from beneath him and down the black top. The sight surreal; like a scene from one of his novels.

"Sam. Sarah. Stay in the car."

"Is he dead?" Sarah's horrified question followed York into the pouring rain.

He suspected he'd found the recipient of the gunshot before he knelt beside the man. York rolled him over.

A blackened hole sat in the center of the victim's forehead.

York gasped and scrambled backwards, landing in a puddle. He dealt with violent death in his novels; he never expected to outside the pages of his latest book. Words did not compare with the stark reality, and York took a deep breath to settle his stomach. He scanned the trees around them.

Was the shooter still out there watching him and the children, or had the driver of the speeding car been the culprit? "Sam! Get my cell phone out of the glove department and call 9-1-1."

"There's no bars up here."

York closed his eyes. *I need a little help here, God.* He couldn't leave the man lying in the middle of the road, and he certainly couldn't stay here so

Sam and Sarah could stare at a corpse.

"Wow." Sam leaned over York's shoulder.

"Get back in the truck." York pushed to his feet. He needed to let the police know about the body. His concern over Darcie battled against the desire to do the right thing.

"I've never seen a dead body before." Sam lifted a pale, rain-streaked face to his father. "Is this what mom looked like?"

"Go. To. Your. Sister." York clenched his jaw.

Sam kicked at the puddle. "I just wanted to help. You treat me like a baby."

York shook his head and watched as Sam joined Sarah in the cab, their faces distorted through the streaming window. He forced a smile to his lips then wiped his sodden hair out of his face. He had one of two choices. Roll the body in the ditch and inform the police of its whereabouts once he got home or load the dead man into the bed of the truck and take him into town himself. Both bad ideas for more reasons than one. The top bad reason would be disturbing a crime scene.

Another glance at Sam and Sarah made up his mind. He grabbed the man's ankles and dragged him to the side of the road. His children had already seen way more than they needed to. After rolling him into the ditch, York piled soggy leaves over the body then sloshed his way back to the truck.

"Are we just going to leave him here?" Tears streamed down Sarah's face.

York turned to face her. "What would you have me do?"

"I don't know. Take him with us."

York puffed out his cheeks and exhaled. "I thought of that, sweetheart, but I…don't know. We still need to find Darcie." He faced forward and pounded the steering wheel.

If he was writing, he'd know exactly what to do. Fiction had nothing on real life. "We'll call the police as soon as we get a signal, okay? Sam, keep an eye on the phone."

"Sure thing." Sam settled back into his seat, York's cell phone clutched in his fist.

York pulled the truck back into the center of the road. He kept an anxious eye on the roiling storm clouds. The thunder boomed like a boiling alley. The lightning blasted across the sky with increasing intensity.

He hadn't driven half a mile before he turned around and parked beside the spot he'd hidden the body. His conscious wouldn't allow him to leave the stranger dumped like garbage.

~

The rain's intensity against Darcie's exposed skin stung as severely as the pile of fire ants she had wandered into as a child. She had to get out of the tree before lightning turned her to toast.

She lay on her belly and scooted until her legs dangled over the side of the tree house. The rough planks dug into her stomach, constricting her breathing. She glanced down. How far could it be? Ten feet, twenty, or more? What's the worst that could happen besides a broken leg? Darcie gulped, closed her eyes, and scooted farther back. Either risk a broken bone, or become a lightning statistic.

A gunshot echoed across the mountain.

Darcie screamed and slipped. She grappled for the nearest board. A splinter drove into her hand, and she hissed against the pain.

Okay, here goes. One, two…she shrieked as she plummeted to the ground and landed with a heavy thud. Thank goodness the soaked ground provided a semblance of cushioning. She lay like a stranded fish fighting for air before struggling to her feet. Nothing seemed broken, although her ankle throbbed with a fiery heat.

With a deep breath, she hobbled through the woods, slapping wet branches away from her face. If crazy people were hunting during a storm, she wanted the safety of her car, meager though it might be. She leaned against another tree to rest her ankle. It would take her all day to get back to her car at this rate.

"Darcie!"

"York!" She limped faster. Relief flooded through her at the sound of his voice. "I'm here."

He burst through the trees and caught her in his arms as her legs lost their strength. With a finger on her chin, York tilted her face upward. "What in the world are you doing out here?"

"Uh, I was, um, revisiting old haunts?"

His eyes hardened. "Do you realize how worried the children and I have been? What possessed you to go wandering through the woods during a storm?"

Darcie pulled free from his hold. "It wasn't storming when I got here. Besides, it's my day off. I didn't think I had to account for my whereabouts." She trudged through mud and leaves back toward the house. She supposed she ought to feel grateful he'd taken the time to look for her. "Thanks for coming after me."

York followed. "You're welcome. Is this where you used to live?"

"Yep. Glorious, isn't it?" She glanced at his muddy jeans and stained shirt. "Is that blood?"

York grabbed her hand. "I'll explain later. I hope you know where we might take shelter." He dragged her at a run.

Pain radiated from her ankle as she struggled to keep up. Darcie glanced to the sky. The rain had stopped and the sky took on a greenish tinge. The trees stilled their rustling.

Clouds swirled anew by the time they reached the truck. York released her hand and yanked open the door. "Come on, you guys. Out. Quick."

Darcie pulled Sarah over the seat. "Is it a tornado?" Her heart constricted as the wind increased, blowing with enough intensity to swirl the damp leaves around her feet.

York peered into her face. "Think, Darcie. We need a place to go."

"Do tornadoes strike on top of a mountain?"

His brows pulled together. "Think faster. Twister or not, the wind is going to be fierce."

She swallowed, hard. "There's a cave not far from here. If I can remember where it is." She turned. The wind whipped her hair around her face, stinging her eyes. "This way." She led them north at a trot. *Where was it?*

Terror choked her as she clutched Sarah's hand. The little girl's wide eyes seemed to swallow her face, jolting Darcie to the severity of their predicament.

She spotted the small enclave in the side of a hill. "Here."

York pushed aside branches and shoved them inside. "Get as far back as you can."

"What if there's an animal in here?" Darcie wrapped her arms around Sam and Sarah.

York laughed. "Are you really worried about that now?"

"Well, yes." Darcie pressed against the packed dirt wall of the cave. She definitely didn't relish fighting an angry mountain lion over the meager space.

The only light came through the furiously waving branches outside, casting York's face in a spider web of black and tan. The cave's corners seemed to disappear into nothingness. She willed her breathing to slow. Surely if an animal waited, it would have made its presence known by now.

"I'm scared." Sarah scooted her trembling body closer to Darcie.

"We'll be fine." Darcie hugged her. "Your daddy will take care of us."

The wind roared louder, making conversation impossible. York joined them and wrapped an arm around Sam.

Darcie's gaze focused on the swirling world outside. A tree fell across the entrance, casting them in darkness. Sarah screamed. The sound ripped away and swirled with the madness surrounding them.

Darcie wanted to copy her. Scream out her fear

and clap her hands over her ears to shut out the horror. She tried to make out York's face. The contour's of his cheeks and chin were dark and in shadow. Then, as quickly as it had begun, the storm ended. Sunlight squeezed through the branches of a tree blocking the cave entrance.

York crawled forward. "I think we can squeeze through. If we work together, we might be able to push the tree away."

Sam joined him and grunted as they shoved against the trunk. "Won't work, Dad. Have Sarah go first. She's the littlest."

He shook his head. "I won't have your sister stuck outside alone if the rest of us can't get out."

A twig snapped outside their prison. Call it instinct or woman's intuition but Darcie clapped a hand over Sarah's mouth. "Shhh."

They all glanced at her, and Darcie pointed.

York placed a hand on his son's shoulder and turned to look outside. A man stood with his back to them, a gun clutched in his fist.

# CHAPTER THIRTEEN

They huddled in the dark like cornered animals. The rain water dripping off leaves masked the sound of their breathing. Darcie eased her hold on Sarah's mouth, silently imploring the little girl to remain quiet and still. An eternity seemed to pass before the man cursed and moved on.

York gripped Darcie's arm and leaned his mouth next to her ear. "You *will* tell me what is going on as soon as we get home." He released her and moved to peer through the branches of the fallen tree. He broke off as much as he could, then squeezed his body out of the cave, leaving a large piece of his shirt behind.

"Wait a minute," he whispered then crawled away. A few long minutes later, he reappeared. "Coast seems clear."

The children scooted, followed by Darcie. Her tee shirt caught on a limb, and she pulled. The fabric ripped, exposing her ribcage to the summer breeze. She slapped the clinging branch away. It swung back, scratching her face. She swiped at her cheek then stared at the smear of blood on her fingers.

Her heart sank like a stone. She knew revealing her secrets had been inevitable. She even suspected, no, she knew, York and the children might be in danger because of her, but despite the evidence, she'd hoped with all within her that it wouldn't be the case. For the first time since her grandmother's death, Darcie felt part of a normal family.

Tears rolled down her face. A family she'd jeopardized by entertaining the thought of staying.

That's exactly what she'd been doing. Baking cookies, bringing home the kittens. She'd been entrenching herself into the daily life of the Wardells. York's finger snapping brought her back to the present.

"The gun man is still out here." He pushed the children ahead of him. "I'd like to get the children to safety."

They trudged silently back to the shack, Darcie's stomach sinking farther with each step. When they reached the clearing she sagged against the house and stared at her Impala. All four tires had been slashed and the front window shattered.

"Get in the truck." York almost growled the words at her.

She didn't blame him, really. If not for her quest, they wouldn't have been stuck on the top of a mountain during a storm and hiding from a man with a gun. The thing was, York didn't even know why. Tears welled in Darcie's eyes. She wasn't too sure herself. The inevitable loomed on the near horizon.

Where would she run this time? If she couldn't be close to this mountain, she'd never find whatever Tony had hidden.

"We have a dead body in the back of the truck." Sarah spoke from the back seat.

Darcie jerked. "What?"

"Yeah, shot right through the head," Sam informed her.

"That's enough." York turned the key in the ignition and shifted the vehicle into four-wheel drive. They bounced their way over fallen trees and back to the mountain road.

Despite herself, Darcie glanced behind them. She made out the toe of a black leather shoe and swallowed against the bile rising in her throat. "What are we going to do with him? Did you shoot him?"

"No, I did not." York shot a cold glance her way. "We'll drop him off at the police station. Unless you have a better suggestion? Maybe we should take him home with us so the man with the gun can follow."

"I'm sorry." Darcie stared at her folded hands.

What if that man had found them cornered like animals? Would he have shot only her or the children too? Would he have shot her at all? Maybe he would have taken her, hoping she knew where Tony's secret was hidden.

"I'm not sure that's good enough." The truck's tires squealed as York rounded a corner too sharply.

He exhaled loudly, and slowed down. "You'd better have one doozy of a story, Darcie Thayer."

Darcie almost laughed at how right he was. She stared out the window the rest of the way to town, taking in the uprooted trees and scattered debris. It didn't appear as if the twister had struck Shadow Springs head-on but the side-swipe left its share of damage in the outlying areas.

Maybe she should have stayed in the tree house. Maybe then God could have struck her with lightning from His right hand, and it would've all been over in the blink of an eye. She glanced over her shoulder at the beautiful faces of Sam and Sarah. She had no right to endanger these precious children, or the man sitting next to her. In the morning, Darcie vowed to leave the sprawling log cabin and its inhabitants behind. Suffering delusions of happiness would only leave others dead.

York parked in front of the small police station. "Stay here. I'll be back in a minute."

~

York shoved through the swinging glass doors of the police station with enough force to slam the door against the wall. Darcie knew something about the dead man and the one who'd wielded a weapon. He intended to find out exactly what her involvement entailed and how much danger his children were in.

"I need to see an officer." York approached a middle-aged woman sitting behind a reception desk.

"Is this an emergency?" She peered at him over glasses perched on her nose.

"If you count having a dead body in the back of

my truck an emergency."

"Oh. Yes. Let me get you someone." She punched a button on her phone and whispered into the receiver. Finished, she glanced back at York. "An officer will be right with you."

York took a step toward a row of plastic chairs when an acquaintance from high school, Roger Downs, approached at a brisk pace. He held out a hand. "York, seems you have something for me."

"Yes, sir." York returned the shake. "I found a body in the middle of High Pass Road. Right at that hair pin turn close to the top. He'd been shot through the forehead."

"Should've left him and called us. It's going to be hard to gather evidence now. Especially after that storm."

"I know that, Roger. I went so far as to roll him in the ditch and cover him with leaves." York ran a hand through his hair. "But I couldn't do it. The kids wouldn't let me."

"How long ago was this?"

"Less than an hour." York waved a hand toward his truck bed.

"You didn't even cover him up?" Roger's eyes widened and he shoved his hat farther back on his head.

York sighed. "I didn't have a tarp. A dead body isn't something you expect to find on your routine afternoon out with the kids. Can you take him or not? It's been a rough day."

"Not as rough as his." Roger clapped York on the shoulder. "Cop humor. I'll call the medical examiner, and we'll have him out of there soon. Did you see anything?"

York filled Roger in on the speeding sedan and the man outside the cave. He debated about telling Roger his suspicions regarding Darcie then decided against it. At least for the time being, until he could find out what she hid behind that angelic face. Darcie could very well be the victim.

Roger slapped his hat back on his head and crossed his arms. "Can't say as I recall any strangers new to town. Things have been as peaceful as always around here."

Yeah, until Darcie showed up on his doorstep. York leaned against his truck and avoided looking in the back. He could sense Darcie and the children watching him. *Lord, make this quick. Don't let my children be around death any longer than necessary.*

"Darcie." York opened the passenger side door. "Take the kids for a soda, would you? Let me take care of things here."

"But, we're filthy." Darcie wiped at a streak of mud on her jeans. "And my shirt is ripped."

"Please."

She nodded and climbed from the seat then stepped aside to let Sam and Sarah out. "How about a drink?" They smiled shakily at York then allowed Darcie to usher them across the street.

"What aren't you telling me, York?" Roger asked.

"I don't know. Darcie's tires were slashed and the window of her Impala smashed while we hid in that cave. There's something she isn't telling me."

When would the medical examiner arrive? The

presence of the corpse gave York the heebie-jeebies.

"Want me to haul her in and question her?"

"No, I'll find out myself."

"Do you think she's involved in anything illegal? If she is, it'd be better if you let me take care of it." Roger laid a hand on his shoulder. "Don't get involved in anything that might cause bad consequences for your family."

Too late for that. York shrugged. "I don't think Darcie's the threat. I think she's in danger and hiding something."

"Well, you know where I'm at if you need me."

A half-hour later with the body removed, York strode across the street and collected Darcie and the kids. They drove home in silence, the children falling asleep even though the sun hadn't fully set.

York sighed and snuck a glance out of the corner of his eye. Darcie twisted the hem of her tee shirt. Good. Let her be nervous. What was with his ability to get involved with devious women? Less than two weeks had passed, but he honestly thought maybe he could have had something with Darcie. Fool.

At home, he shook Sam awake and gathered Sarah in his arms. He glanced back at Darcie. "I'll get these two on the sofa until dinner's ready. Just use one of the casseroles in the freezer." Day off or not, she owed him and his exhausted children something to eat at least.

Then, after Sam and Sarah were fed, bathed, and tucked into bed, he'd get to the bottom of Darcie's secrets.

# CHAPTER FOURTEEN

Darcie hid behind the sleepy murmurings of Sam and Sarah as she helped them get ready for bed. She couldn't escape York's steely side-ways glances. Who would have thought dark chocolate eyes could appear so cold?

Children kissed and tucked beneath the covers, Darcie sighed and closed the door. She met York's gaze then led the way down the stairs and to the back porch. The man's resolve at waiting was iron-clad. He leaned against the railing and crossed his arms. His eyes glittered behind his glasses.

Wow. Darcie plopped into a rocking chair and gnawed her lower lip. York would hate her when she finished. No help for it. She'd have to sacrifice what might have been for what was. And that was her need to find Tony's package. Fast. "I don't know where to start."

"The beginning?" His sarcasm increased

Darcie's nervousness.

The butterflies in her stomach grew to the size of elephants. She took a deep breath and released it loudly, her hand brushing across her belly. "My late husband, Tony, had a, uh, gambling problem, to put it mildly. He got involved with a group of men who laundered money. At least that's the best I can figure out. We argued about it the night he died. I took my eyes off the road and crashed into a tree. I lost Tony and my unborn child that night." She swallowed against the lump rising in her throat.

York uncrossed his arms but kept his spot across the porch from her. "What does that have to do with what happened today?"

Did he have to be so cruel, so heartless? "Before Tony died, he said he hid something in a shack. Or by one." Darcie shrugged. "I'm not exactly sure anymore. I'm assuming he meant here in Shadow Springs. This is where we're both from. He said the package would keep me safe."

"What is it?"

"I don't know. I can't find it." She peered through the growing darkness trying to register how York accepted the information. "I really didn't mean to involve you or the kids."

"How did these men find you? Do you know the man who's body we found?"

"I don't know who he is, and I don't know what they're searching for."

"That part's obvious. They're waiting for you to find what your husband hid so they can take it." York rolled his head on his shoulders then paced the porch. "I'm sorry about your husband and baby. I really am, but this load of trouble you've brought to my doorstep is hard to digest." He stopped in front of her. "Why me?"

"You were a job. A way to make money that's close to where I need to be looking." Darcie clasped her hands tight enough together to make her knuckles ache. "I'll pack my things and leave in the morning."

He placed his hands on the arms of the chair and leaned close enough she could smell his musky after shave and feel his breath on her face. "Am I still *just* a job to you, Darcie?"

"Yes, I mean no, I…" she whispered. "You're an answer to a means." She raised her chin. "I've grown to care for you, Sam, and Sarah, but staying here will bring danger to you."

Care for him? Her feelings bordered on love, and she knew it. What would York do with her love? Would he deceive her as Tony had done? No, she couldn't admit her growing feelings, even if it might pave the way for her to stay.

He laughed, the sound hard. "You've already done that, sweetheart." York straightened. "You might as well go to bed. We have a barbecue to go to tomorrow."

"What?"

"Suzy is having a barbecue. Might be a good time to see whether there are any strangers in town. Other than our dead friend, anyway. You've been here less than two weeks and have managed to turn our lives upside down."

"I'm sorry." A barbecue? The answers Darcie gave him had driven him over the edge. If she remembered correctly, Suzy's get-to-gathers involved most of the town. Darcie would be a sitting duck. Maybe that was his plan. A way to get her out of his hair without him having to be the bad guy.

She rose and tried to slip past York. He grabbed her arm and yanked her to him, lowering his mouth to hers. His lip-bruising kiss rocked her world, making her legs weak. She sagged against him.

He released her abruptly.

Using the wall for support, she gasped. Her senses reeled. Her lips burned.

"Am I *still* just a job to you, Darcie?"

She wanted to say no. But making York aware of her growing feelings for him would only make him think he needed to take care of her. He didn't. His children were his main concern. Not some ignorant girl from the wrong side of the mountain who'd gotten herself involved in something over her head.

Tears stung her eyes and she opened her mouth to hiss, "Yes."

~

York leaped from the porch and marched around the corner of the house. What was wrong with him? He'd never used the heavy-handed approach with a woman before.

Just a job? He didn't believe her for a moment. Not with the way she'd responded to his kiss. He laughed, the sound raw and forced.

If he were writing the scene for his novel, he'd turn around and make her see the truth about her feelings. He wasn't an idiot. He knew what the hungry gazes she sent his way meant. Darcie

Thayer cared for him and his children more than she'd admit to anyone. The woman might be spitting mad at him for the way he'd treated her, but a fire lurked behind those pain-filled golden eyes.

He kept moving until he entered the trees bordering his property. York kicked at a stump. The dead wood collapsed beneath the weight of his foot. *God, what do you want me to do?* He felt for certain Darcie didn't share his faith, meager though it might be at times. *What more do You want me to take?*

First Michelle's betrayal, now this.

York shoved his hands through his hair. This involved his children.

Would the men who followed Darcie be content with her, or would they go after York and the kids? Ugh! Think, man. Could he let Darcie go off and fend for herself knowing how he was starting to feel about her?

He didn't know how long he stood in the dark, railing at God, and trying to formulate a plan out of his rambling thoughts. The squeak of the screen door brought him back to the problems at hand.

Through the trees, he could make out Darcie leaning against the wall of the house. The kitten pounced around her feet, and she stooped to scoop it into her arms. He sighed, knowing he'd have to apologize for the rough kiss.

Darcie dropped the kitten and ducked back inside when a car sounded on the road in front of the house. Her jittery behavior made sense now. The woman acted scared of her shadow. And for good reason. She might put up a tough front, but she needed someone to look after her. Did he want the job?

He had no reason to believe the ones following her knew her exact location. Just that she'd gone back to Shadow Springs. They seemed to know where she'd grown up but not where she lived now. At least he hoped so. He prayed he could help her and keep the strangers at bay.

The cars that he'd seen slow in front of this house seemed more like they searched for something rather than they'd found what they looked for. He'd like to think that if they knew for sure where Darcie was, they would have acted long before now.

He gnawed the inside of his cheek. Shack didn't necessarily mean the one she grew up in. There had to be several buildings on the mountain worthy of the title. Monday, he's ask Mrs Olsen to watch Sam and Sarah and he'd help Darcie find the…whatever it was her husband had hidden.

With heavy steps, he made his way back to the house. The aroma of coffee greeted him at the back door. Through the window he spotted Darcie at the kitchen table. She brushed a finger across her lips. He smiled, knowing she'd been as affected by the kiss as he had.

He pushed the door open. She lifted her head at the squeak of the hinges. A wary glance at him made York's heart clench.

"I'm sorry." He strode quickly to her side. "I didn't mean to react that way." He grabbed her hands and pulled her to her feet. "You should've told me."

"Would you have hired me if I had?"

"Probably not."

They laughed, and York pulled her gently to his chest. "I'd like to try and help. Monday, when Mrs. Olsen is here, I'll search with you. Then, I'll send the children home with her for a few days. She still keeps a house on the other side of the mountain."

"Really?" His heart leaped at the hopeful expression on her face.

York nodded. "Let's find this thing and get rid of it."

"Are you sure? They came for me in the hospital after the accident. The nurses wouldn't allow visitors, and my head was bandaged. They still thought I was unconscious but I heard strangers asking about Darcie Thayer. I'm not sure they know exactly what I look like but you could be in danger. The kids could be…"

He put his fingers over her mouth. "Trust God, Darcie. I'm sure they just want what they perceive to be theirs. Let's give it to them."

She laid her head beneath his chin. "Thank you. I'm tired of fighting on my own."

"Come here." York took her by the hand and led her to the living room. "Sit. Let me get the coffee. There's something I need to talk to you about."

Before they went any further, he needed to broach the subject of God, whether Darcie wanted to hear it or not. He filled two mugs with fragrant brew then carried them in and sat next to her. He handed Darcie a mug. "Better take a good strong sip."

"Goodness, what is it? You can't have anything

worse to say than I did."

York rotated his shoulders. "You brought up a good point about possible dangers. I'd like to ask where you stand with God."

"Nowhere." Her lips thinned. "He took my younger brother from my arms. God has no time for me, nor I for him."

York grinned. "So, you do acknowledge He exists."

"Of course He exists! I'm not stupid." Darcie set her mug on the coffee table and jumped to her feet. "God has taken away everything important to me."

"God didn't. Man did."

She whirled to face him. Her gaze shot daggers. "Man did not give my baby brother pneumonia or allow him to die in my arms from it."

York was reminded of Jesus telling the disciples that a demon couldn't be removed without prayer. Darcie Thayer's past was riddled with pain and the pain demons needed a lot of prayer. He smiled, admiring her spunk, and propped crossed ankles on the table top. "I value your opinion, Darcie. But I believe God has a purpose and a reason for everything. So, if I'm going to help you, we do it my way. By asking and relying on God."

She waved a hand. "Whatever. When we wind up dead, you can ask God where he was!"

# CHAPTER FIFTEEN

The next day, the summer morning shined brighter but failed to dispel Darcie's dark mood. She'd discovered nothing by returning to the town she grew up in. Each night, she laid in bed fuming over York's attempts to "religionize" her, as she called it. Daylight hours were spent entertaining Sam and Sarah.

Her grandmother regaled her with tales of Bible heroes when she'd moved in with her. Darcie even accompanied her to church every weekend, going so far as accepting salvation. But the dark cloud of despair and depression that hung over her until Tony entered the picture, kept out all thoughts of God's loving kindness. Darcie had seen anything but. If that was what being saved meant, she no longer wanted it.

She shouldn't have said anything.

Disappearing with York none the wiser would've

been the best option. She dumped the pot of boiled potatoes into the colander. Hot water splashed over her hand, and she hissed against the burn. She slammed on the cold water faucet and let it run, soothing the pain.

Making her famous potato salad didn't hold the enjoyment it normally did. Not if she had to take it to Suzy's and pretend life was grand.

Thundering footsteps signaled the arrival of the children. She directed them to the table where honey and homemade biscuits waited. She glanced at the ceiling.

Would York make an appearance anytime soon or was he trying to squeeze in a few minutes of writing? She shrugged. What he did with his time was his business.

The children ate and dashed outside before York made his appearance. Darcie stashed the salad in the refrigerator and set a plate of fresh biscuits on the table.

York entered the kitchen and raised an eyebrow as he took his seat.

"Not my job, I know." Darcie shrugged. "But I don't care for cold cereal much and if I'm cooking for myself, I might as well make enough for everyone, and it is Mrs. Olsen's day off."

"I appreciate it. These are great. Stick around long enough and I might have to fire Mrs. Olsen." York squirted a heavy dose of honey on his biscuit. "With her getting on in years, I have her cook breakfast less often and spend more time at her own house."

Drowning her with charm wouldn't work.

Neither would good looks. Darcie tore her gaze away from the way his biceps strained against the fabric of his tee shirt. Authors weren't supposed to be buff, were they? They sat behind a computer all day.

"Suzy has a pool if you like to swim." York shoved the last of his breakfast in his mouth and rose. "I'll get the kids." He shook his head. "I never could figure out why Suzy's parties have to last more than a few hours. It starts right after church and most likely won't end until past dark."

Church! He hadn't said anything about her having to attend with them. She didn't, did she?

He glanced at her flowered sundress. "What you're wearing is fine. We aren't formal."

He *did* intend for her to accompany him. Darcie shrugged. She'd dealt with worse. Sitting in a stuffy pew with turned-up nosed people wouldn't kill her. But spending all day with Suzy Boushee might.

York hauled in an ice chest and a bag of ice.

Darcie laid the salad and sodas inside it then followed while York carried the cooler to his truck. He gave her a wink and held open the door. "Ready? God awaits."

Darcie rolled her eyes and climbed into the passenger side.

When they pulled into the parking lot of the small country church, Darcie expected a sign to flash above her head, proclaiming skeptic, sinner, or worse. Instead, the parishioners greeted her with smiles and handshakes.

A couple of older women remembered her grandmother and expressed thoughts on how much they missed her. Feeling surprised and overwhelmed, Darcie blinked back tears and allowed York to tuck her hand in the crook of his arm and lead her inside.

Sam and Sarah raced off to what Darcie presumed would be their Sunday school classes while she and York took seats toward the back of the sanctuary. A band struck a note, and she found herself blown away by a contemporary style of worship that sang to God instead of about him. Her stomach fluttered, and she swallowed against the universe-sized lump in her throat.

To make things more uncomfortable, the pastor started teaching on God knocking on the door of people's hearts and them answering. Darcie plucked at the skirt of her dress. She felt York watching from the corner of his eye and struggled to compose herself.

Darcie glared then focused on her hands folded in her lap. She'd heard God plenty of times. He didn't usually have anything she wanted to hear. First an abusive mother with scores of "uncles", her neglected brother dying of pneumonia, Tony's deceitful promise, now she was on the run again. Did God have *any* good news for Darcie Thayer?

~

York couldn't help it. He enjoyed Darcie's squirming next to him. Being uncomfortable in church usually meant God was trying to get your attention. And if there was one woman who needed to acknowledge Him, it was Darcie. He smiled at her discomfort and turned his attention back to the pastor who said a blessing over the congregation then dismissed them.

Darcie's gaze seemed constantly scanning as they made their way to the children's classrooms. Despite York's firm grip of her elbow, she avoided his eyes, keeping a firmness around her mouth and a stiffness to her spine.

"Relax. You survived."

Darcie took a deep breath. "I'm not nervous about being in church, York. That's over. I'm keeping a look-out for anyone overly interested in me."

"Besides all the old ladies who knew your grandmother?" He scrawled his name on the Sunday School sign-out sheet and smiled at Sam and Sarah as they dashed to his side.

York spotted Mrs. Olsen speaking with the pastor's wife and asked Darcie and the kids to stay in the foyer where he could see them. He waved to catch his housekeeper's attention and strode to her side.

"Can I speak with you for a minute?"

"Sure, York." Mrs. Olsen smiled at the woman she'd been talking to then turned to York. "What's up?"

How did he begin? "Remember your suspicions about Darcie being in some kind of trouble?"

She frowned. "I was right, wasn't I?"

"Yes." York lowered his voice. "It has to do with her late husband. Anyway, I'd like to help her get things sorted out. Could you watch Sam and Sarah for the next week? At your brother's house, preferably?" Her home would leave them without a man's protection.

Mrs. Olsen squared her shoulders. "And leave you and Darcie without any chaperone at all? That would not look good."

"I'm not really concerned about that." York ran a hand through his hair.

"You should be." Mrs. Olsen set fists on her hips. "You can drop the children off in the morning and pick all of us up in the evenings. That's the best I can do. If Darcie's in enough trouble that you have to be concerned with the children's safety, then you should go to the police. Better yet, I could stay at your place as usual."

"I have a feeling my house is being watched."

Uncomfortable with how close his side of the conversation came to lying, York jammed his hands in his pockets, then pulled them out and crossed his arms. "We have to find something that Tony hid either at Darcie's mom's house or her grandmother's. Once we find it, I'll take it to the police myself."

"Does Darcie know that's your plan?"

He glanced at the subject of their conversation. "Partially."

"Uh-huh. I doubt she'd be very happy." Mrs. Olsen poked him in the chest with her forefinger. "You're falling for that girl, York Wardell. Don't let it cloud your judgment."

He gave her a mock salute. "Yes, ma'am." As he turned, he commented over his shoulder, "Oh, and could you keep an eye out for any strangers in town?"

"What?"

"Anyone new to town. Men in particular. Let me

know if you see any." He patted her shoulder then made his way to the waiting three-some and escorted them back to the truck. Once he'd climbed behind the wheel, he turned to his kids. "Mrs. Olsen is going to be watching you this week. I've got to help Darcie take care of some family business."

"Mrs. Olsen!" Sam slammed back in his seat. "I'll be bored out of my mind."

"We'll bake cookies." Sarah clicked her seatbelt. "I won't mind that."

"It's only for a few days." York turned the key in the ignition. "You'll survive."

Darcie snorted. "Is that your answer to everything? You'll survive?"

"Yep." York maneuvered the truck from the parking space and headed toward Suzy's house. He hoped Darcie's attitude improved. Things would be difficult enough with his having to escape the scarlet talons of Suzy without having to dodge Darcie's barbs as well.

If they only knew more about Tony's so-called package. Was it larger than a hard-bound book? More like an envelope? Or bigger still? Knowing the size would help pin-point a possible hiding place. Something small could be anywhere. Including beneath the proverbial hay stack. York sighed. He'd give her a week before he called the police and let them worry about the unknown man with a gun.

# CHAPTER SIXTEEN

York fought back a grimace as Susy Bouchee sashayed up and plastered herself to his arm the minute he and Darcie arrived. Despite the ice chest he carried, Suzy grabbed his elbow with both hands and dragged him with her to the buffet tables. He glanced over his shoulder. Darcie grinned with as much humor as a shark.

"Don't worry about me and the kids. We'll be fine over by the pool." Darcie gave him a little wave and marched off.

"Wait, I, uh…" York felt like a child deserted by his best friend and left with the neighborhood bully.

"They'll be fine." Suzy smiled up at him. "There's no reason for you to spend every waking minute with your children's nanny."

"I suppose not." But what if he wanted to? He shrugged free of her grip and hefted the cooler more securely in his arms. "Where do you want this?"

"Let's put it over by the buffet tables. One's for drinks, the other for food. I've got a whole pig roasting over the fire, and I've hired a bartender so the fun can go on all night." She ran a finger down his cheek.

"I don't drink." York set the cooler beneath a table and lifted the lid.

"You're such a stick in the mud. I can run everyone off earlier if you'd like." She batted her lashes at him. "Then we could spend some alone time."

York rolled his eyes and tightened his lips before setting the potato salad on the table and reaching for a soda. Anything to keep his hands occupied. Staying busy might be his only defense against the blond piranha. "I don't like Sam and Sarah staying up too late. I'll get them home at a reasonable time."

"That is what the nanny is for." Suzy pouted. "Work with me here. Why, if I didn't know better…"

"Miss Bouchee?" One of the bartenders interrupted.

"Excuse me." Suzy stepped away, firing instructions regarding the drinks she wanted served.

York relaxed and scoured the sloping lawn for Darcie. She sat on the edge of the sparkling pool, dress drawn above her knees, soda in hand, and feet in the water. He wanted to sit next to her, put an arm around her shoulders, and pretend, for the moment, they were a couple. Not employer and employee.

The sun shone on her head, highlighting her hair

with fire. Touching her would burn as bad as dunking his arm elbow deep in hot water.

He shook his head. If someone would've told him a year ago he'd be falling for another woman, he would've told them to jump in the lake. Darcie and his wife, Michelle, couldn't be more different. Darcie shined warm and golden, where Michelle had been more refined. Controlled. Cool.

He shifted his gaze. Sam and Sarah played a game of tag with a group of other children. He continued to scan the grounds, looking for anyone out of the ordinary. Someone who paid too much attention to the single women mingling around. He'd begun to suspect the men following Darcie weren't sure where she hid. Just that she was in Shadow Springs somewhere. Did they even know what she looked like? Probably not or they would've taken her by now.

He shook his head. Cars up and down the mountain at every hour of the night. Slowing, then speeding up. The guy around Darcie's family home. None of it made sense to him. Were they checking every newly arrived female in town or just her?

The activity on the mountain road told him they must suspect she was there somewhere. No one lived on his particular road. Shivers slipped up his spine. What kind of game were these men playing?

Women stood in clusters, chattering or calling after children. Men lounged in groups spouting tall tales. Most of them York recognized, although a few were strangers. These were the ones he wanted to keep an eye on.

Two men he didn't know kept their gazes on

Suzy as she flitted from one circle of guests to another. One short and dark, the other tall and light, balding. Suzy glowed with the attention, often sending the men coy looks as she worked her way to them, chattering with her guests as she passed.

The way they watched her made York nervous. Like predators eyeing their prey. Fond of the woman or not, he moved closer, making sure he kept Darcie in sight as well.

Suzy giggled and leaned toward one of the strangers. "Sure, I'm a native. Just got back to town a bit ago. You can take the girl out of the country, but you can't take the country out of the girl."

"Southern belles have the most beautiful accents," one of them said.

"Oh, you do flatter me." Suzy flipped her hair. "The big city wasn't for me. It's great to be home."

York rolled his eyes and tried to act casual, keeping his ears tuned and his gaze anywhere but on the flirting trio. He couldn't help but feel relieved to see Suzy's attention diverted off him.

His heart skipped a beat when one of the men excused himself and went to speak to Darcie. She shrugged him off with a cold glance. York smiled and took another sip of his drink. The sprite could take care of herself it seemed.

Sarah dashed up to Darcie, and she rose to follow the little girl. York laughed when Darcie joined in a game of Red Rover. She giggled when she burst through the line of the opposing team, and York wished his daughter would've invited him as well.

He turned back to Suzy. She and her gentlemen friends were nowhere to be seen.

~

Darcie lifted her skirt high enough to run and sprinted to the opposing team breaking through easily. She laughed, feeling like a little girl, and chose a shy child to accompany her back.

She glanced up. York watched her over the rim of his plastic cup. Her face heated. He must think her silly, running with the children, but she couldn't remember the last time she'd been so carefree. Tony's package hung over her head, promising to wait until maturity set back in.

Winded, she bowed out of the next game and strolled toward the buffet tables laden with food and drink. Laughter surrounded her, along with the sounds of children shrieking, water splashing, and music playing from a hidden stereo. She grabbed a can of soda and sighed.

Why couldn't her life be as simple; as ideal? She wanted barbecues to be the norm, not one moment away from the terror of her life. She glanced at York who still watched with dark, hooded eyes. Darcie wanted *that*. Or at least something like it. She wanted a man who watched her as if she were everything to him.

Where was Suzy? The woman seemed strangely absent at her own party, and Darcie couldn't help but feel relieved not to have to dodge the other woman's hidden innuendos about Darcie's status in life, or lack thereof. She supposed she ought to mingle and try to discover any strangers to town, but being newly arrived herself, she wouldn't know who'd lived here for a while and who hadn't.

"Hey, pretty lady." She turned and glared at a

man barely taller than she. Buff arms stretched the fabric of the man's button-up shirt. "Haven't seen you around these parts before."

"I've been around for a long time." Darcie's turned and nodded at York.

His long strides carried him quickly to her side. "Hey, Sweetheart, who's your friend?"

"Um, this is…" Darcie raised an eyebrow at the stranger.

"Sorry." The man raised his hands. "I thought the lady was alone."

"No chance," York smiled. "Our children are over there." He pointed to where Sam and Sarah filled plates with fried chicken and chips.

Darcie breathed a sigh of relief when the man left. "Thanks for rescuing me."

"You did great, not letting on you'd just arrived back in town. If that is our mystery man, he won't know you're the woman he's looking for." York stared after him. "But he does look like one of the men who gathered around Suzy. Where is she?"

"I'm wondering the same thing." Darcie handed him her empty cup. "Let me check the house. Maybe she's in the restroom."

"She keeps the main house locked during her parties. The guesthouse is open."

Really? How would he know? Darcie smirked.

"I've been to other parties here, Darcie. Suzy entertains a lot."

*I'm sure she does.* Darcie made her way toward the smaller, white clapboard building on the edge of the lawn. Although she wasn't anxious to spend time with their hostess, she also knew it wasn't common for Suzy to desert her guests for a long period of time. She enjoyed the attention too much. Maybe she'd taken ill from food set out too long.

A few people milled outside the guesthouse, and a line formed at the restroom. Darcie turned to a room on her left and pushed open the door. "Suzy?"

She stepped into a bedroom and flicked on the light. "Suzy?"

The woman lay on top of a brocade comforter across a pine four-poster bed. One hand dangled over the mattress.

# CHAPTER SEVENTEEN

Darcie stepped closer to the bed, swallowing against the rising lump in her throat. Her hands shook with each violent pound of her heart. The hair on her arms rose as she reached toward the still woman.

A mustard-colored scarf twisted around the other woman's neck. Her blue eyes bulged, focused unseeing on the ceiling fan overhead. Her pale skin held a tinge of blue.

Darcie stumbled back and crashed into a small nightstand. A tiffany lamp fell and shattered on the hardwood floor. They'd found her! They were here. She clapped a hand over her mouth. They got the wrong woman! Wait.

Was it possible someone else had killed Suzy? Maybe it wasn't the same ones chasing Darcie. With Suzy's often abrasive personality and flirty ways, it wasn't inconceivable that someone else would want her out of the picture.

Like fighting against hurricane force winds, Darcie forced herself back to the bed. What if Suzy wasn't dead? Maybe the culprit didn't succeed. Darcie poked Suzy with her forefinger. Cold. She felt for a pulse. Nothing. She jumped back and shook her hand as if that would remove the feel of Suzy's skin. The other woman didn't move. Darcie spun and dashed from the room.

York would know what to do.

She lost a shoe sprinting across the lawn, stooped to retrieve it, then continued her rush to find York. She hoped he'd have a better head on his shoulders than she apparently did. She stopped behind a hedge beside the pool, slipped her foot back into her sandal, then parted the greenery to scan the party goers.

No one seemed aware that their hostess lay dead just yards from them. Darcie covered her head with her hands. She'd seen death before. First her little brother, then Tony. She wanted it gone. Tossed away like sludge.

"I don't think she's the one."

Darcie held her breath at a man's chilly tone.

"It must be that red head."

Another man's voice chimed in. "They should have told us more than she had light hair! That's half the women in this town."

"They told us enough. There are only two women who recently arrived in town with hair of that description. You took care of the one you were responsible for. That leaves the nanny."

Darcie clamped a hand over her mouth to stifle a gasp. Please, God, don't let them hear her.

"But that big guy acted like they was married. They got kids and everything."

"They're lying. They must be on to us. Do you think she's found the package?"

"Doesn't matter one way or the other. Once she's out of the picture, there won't be any worries. If she was going to find it, she would have by now. Maybe there ain't no package. Regardless, we got orders. We wait for an opportunity, and we take it. Just like the floozy back there."

Darcie's blood ran cold. The men spoke casually of killing her as if life didn't matter. Nothing personal, just a job. She blinked back tears. Now was not the time to fall apart.

"Darcie?"

She glanced up then threw herself into York's arms. "Shhh."

He wrapped his arms around her. "What's the matter? What did you find?"

"Suzy. In the guesthouse bedroom. She's dead." Darcie shuddered. "And two men on the other side of these bushes are talking about going after me now."

"What?" York set her back at arm's length.

"With a scarf. Someone strangled her, and now they're coming after me."

"Are you sure?"

Darcie nodded. "I heard them." She trembled, tempted to call upon God to save her. Guilt at eleventh hour praying erased the thought. She needed to feel God's presence at other times, not when she felt compelled to call on Him out of fear.

York shoved her behind him and peered through

the hedge.

~

Mothers sipped iced drinks from lawn chairs where they could watch over the play. Younger men jostled around a make-shift basketball court. Sam and Sarah splashed in the shallow end of the pool with a group of kids around their ages.

"No one's there. At least no one who looks as if they don't belong." He searched for the two men last seen with Suzy.

"They must have left." Darcie grabbed his arm. "Maybe they heard you. What are we going to do?"

He turned to face her. "Are you sure they were talking about you?"

"I'm positive. They said red hair and nanny." Her face paled. "How many nannies do you think Shadow Springs has?" Her voice rose. "It's not a common job up here."

York ran a hand over the stubble on his chin. He needed to get the kids to Mrs. Olsen and get Darcie hidden away. Where? The cabin. Could he do it? He hadn't gone up there since the first year of his marriage. It wasn't common knowledge that he now owned Michelle's family's hunting cabin. He'd never been able to pinpoint why he'd bought the place. Maybe this was it. It ought to be the perfect place and not too far away from where he and Darcie needed to search for the package.

"Come on." He gripped Darcie's hand.

He dragged her with him, called to Sam and Sarah to follow, and marched to his truck. He wrestled with the idea of calling Roger at the police department. What could he tell him of Darcie's involvement? *God, what I am doing? I need wisdom and discernment now more than any other time in my life.*

Poor Suzy. Despite his spurning of her attention, he hadn't wanted the life of that vivacious woman snuffed out as if she had no worth. The best he could do now was to keep Darcie from suffering the same fate.

At this moment, speaking with Roger would waste valuable time in fleeing and possibly tie up Darcie where she couldn't disappear. She'd be held where the killers could easily get to her. Especially now that they'd narrowed their choice of victims. The small precinct at Shadow Springs wouldn't be a deterrent for killers if they wanted to break in and reach someone.

A scream ripped through the early evening. York assumed they'd discovered Suzy's body and increased his pace.

He ushered the children into the truck, despite their protests at leaving so early. He pulled his cell phone from his pocket. His finger hovered over the numbers. Roger would recognize the call as coming from York. He'd have to use a pay phone, but that meant driving to town. If he used Mrs. Olsen's when he dropped off Sam and Sarah, Roger would put the pieces together and still know York called. He shoved the phone back in his pocket. Calling now wasn't an option.

He closed his eyes. *Lord, I'm digging myself a huge hole here. The deeper I get, the harder it'll be to climb out of.*

As he slid behind the wheel of the truck, he

reached again for his phone and glanced through the front windshield. His gaze met that of the smaller of the two men he'd seen speaking with Suzy. He'd have to make the call while driving.

"Get your seatbelts on, guys. We're going for a ride." York twisted the key in the ignition and pressed the gas pedal. The truck lurched from Suzy's driveway.

"York?" Darcie's voice trembled.

"We're being followed. Hold on." He spun the wheel left, taking them onto the paved mountain road. "I know a short cut to Mrs. Olsen's. Sam. Sarah. You're going there tonight."

"But, Daddy, my dolls. My clothes." Sarah gripped the seat with two hands. "Why can't we wait until tomorrow?"

"Please, don't argue. Mrs. Olsen can take you tomorrow to pick up your things."

"If she does that, what if the men are waiting for her?" Darcie laid a hand on his arm.

York's heart froze. He'd have to take the children with them. *God, no*. He glanced over at Darcie's heart-shaped face, tempted to leave her and the dangers that surrounded her in order to spare his children. He couldn't do it. Not anymore. She'd already claimed a piece of his heart. God, help them.

They'd need supplies. The cabin held the bare minimum of anything. Could he chance a quick trip home? No. Mrs. Olsen? The woman would do everything in her power to help him, he knew. But at what risk? With his left hand, he pressed the number to call his housekeeper.

"Hello?"

"Mrs. Olsen? I'm in need of supplies."

She listened quietly as he spoke in terse sentences, saying as little as possible to remind her of their earlier conversation

"I gather you aren't dropping the children off?"

"I can't put you in that position."

"Where are you now?"

"Miller's road. We won't be by until dark. Can you have the things ready? Put them by the mailbox."

"It'll be ready. York, you seriously need to reconsider. The police…"

"Can't help us right now. Once we have what they're looking for, we'll go there immediately. That's all I can promise."

Mrs. Olsen sighed. "Do you need any money?"

"It wouldn't hurt." He laughed. "You know the safe combination, right? If you can spare what you have, then you can reimburse yourself in a day or two. Don't go to the house before then. Please, don't put yourself, or your brother, at risk."

The back window of the truck exploded in a shower of glass.

# CHAPTER EIGHTEEN

Darcie screamed and covered her head from the cascade of glass. Then, she turned, knelt, and leaned over the back of the seat. "Sarah! Sam!"

"Get down!" York swung his arm behind him trying to reach his children. "All of you get down."

Sarah screeched, covered her head, and dove to the floor with her brother.

Another shot rang out, thudding into the truck's tailgate.

Darcie ducked.

A black sedan quickly decreased the amount of distance between them and the truck, looming larger through the frame of the shattered window. The man who'd approached Darcie at the pool hung out of the sedan window, gun leveled in her direction. She slid back down and slouched.

"What are we going to do?" She glanced at York.

"Ditch 'em." He increased their speed.

Rocks pinged the Ford's undercarriage. A cloud of dust engulfed the car behind them. Darcie didn't believe obscurity would stop a mad man's bullet.

"We've got to go faster!"

"I'm…doing…the best I can." York whipped the wheel to the right taking them down what could only be called a trail. "This baby can go where that car can't. I hope."

Sarah's screams continued to split the air until Darcie's nerves rang along with the loud tones. She needed to get back there. She rose and barreled over the seat, landing on the floor next to the little girl. She wrapped her arms around Sarah and used her body as a shield. Sam huddled beside them, hands covering his ears.

"Hold on back there." York's voice rose above the banging rocks and zinging bullets. "It's going to get rough." The truck spun to the left. Darcie slammed against the door.

Branches scratched along the sides like skeletal fingers, whining on their journey of destroying the paint job.

"They're falling behind!" York's jubilant shout raised Darcie's spirits. She shifted to peer out the window.

Sure enough the pursuers were losing ground. She wanted to cry with relief.

De ja vu threatened with the car chase. Terror of York and the children meeting the same fate as Tony ebbed. With the danger of crashing into a tree diminishing, Darcie's heart rate decelerated. Her breathing slowed. "Shhh, baby. It's going to be okay." She smoothed Sarah's hair away from her face with one hand and gripped Sam's with the other. "Your daddy will take care of us." And if God had any mercy left for Darcie, so would He.

"You can get up now. We've lost them." York glanced over the seat then turned back to the front. "Everyone all right?"

Darcie eased the kinks out of her battered body and climbed back to her seat. "We're fine. Sam and Sarah are shook up, but not hurt. How much farther?"

"Maybe ten minutes, if you're a bird. It's tucked away in a little hollow away from everything but God and his creation. We've got to stop and pick up supplies before doing anything. The cabin won't have much. That means a long drive around the mountain then back this way again."

A bead of perspiration ran down York's brow. Darcie wiped it away with her finger. As terrified as she'd been, how much more so had he? It was his children in the backseat. His children she'd put at risk by becoming their nanny.

"I'm sorry."

York frowned. "For what?"

"Dragging you into this." Tears burned Darcie's eyes.

"Too late. We're in it now. You can't do this alone." York shrugged. "We'll be fine. Once we find what you're looking for, we'll turn it over to the police and this will all go away."

She hoped so. Hiding had seemed the best plan a year ago. Jumping from one low paying job to another. Moving from town to town. Darcie shook her head. Then, she'd decided to search for Tony's package and look where it'd gotten her. Smack back in the middle of what she'd been running from.

York dug his cell phone out of his pocket.

"What are you doing?" Darcie turned in her seat.

"Calling Roger."

"You can't call the police!" Was he crazy?

York sighed. "I wasn't going to when we left Suzy's. But I have to. I won't tell him where we're going, and I'll toss the phone when I'm finished."

"If you get rid of the phone, we won't have any way of calling if we're in real trouble."

"You don't call this trouble?" York's brows rose. "I'll keep the phone, is that what you want?"

"I don't know what I want." The welling tears fell. "Except for this to end."

~

York stared in horror as Darcie sobbed. What did she want him to do? He had a hard enough time handling Sarah's tears, much less a grown woman's. He patted her awkwardly on the shoulder. "It'll be okay. Really. I'll get us out of this."

Darcie wiped her tears on the hem of her dress. "I'm fine. Call if you want."

Wow. Confusion reigned supreme. He dialed Roger's number, casting worried glances at Darcie. "Yeah, Roger. Are you at Suzy's yet?"

"How did you know about that?"

"Oh. Well, Darcie is the one who found her." York wanted to close his eyes and lay his head back. This conversation was not going to go well.

Roger let loose a string of expletives. "Are you kidding me? You know you can't leave the scene of a crime! All that research you do for your books ought to tell you that much."

"There are extenuating circumstances. The killers were actually after Darcie. They got the wrong woman."

"Then you need to bring her in so we can protect her."

York shook his head then realized Roger couldn't see him through the air waves. "Not until we find whatever they're looking for. I'm sorry, but I can't do what you're asking. I've got to think of the safety of my children. We were chased from the party at gunpoint."

Roger sighed. "What are you going to do now?"

"Hide out and look for the mysterious package. I'll call you if I need you."

"I don't like this. Not a bit, but I'll keep my phone handy for when you come to your senses. At least give me a description to work with."

"One is about five foot nine and wiry. Dark hair. The other's about my height and weighs about thirty pounds more. Oh, and, Roger. Keep an eye on the Olsens for me, will you?"

"As many as I can spare. Keep me posted when you know more about our killers." Roger hung up without saying goodbye.

"What did he say, Dad?" Sam leaned over the seat.

"We're on our own until we call him." York smiled to take the edge of his words. "How about we get to our cabin? It'll be like a vacation."

The three of them stared at him like he'd lost his mind. Maybe he had.

"But first, we've got to make a stop." York

glanced at the setting sun. Within fifteen minutes it'd be dark enough for him to pull alongside the mailbox, grab the supplies, and zip off with, hopefully, no one the wiser.

"I want to stay with Mrs. Olsen." Sarah crossed her arms and bounced back against the seat. "I don't like this running around and getting shot at. This isn't the movies!"

"We're a family, Sarah." Sam said. "Families stick together. Right, Dad?"

"Right, son." York reached over and grabbed Darcie's hand. "How's it feel to be a Wardell, even for a short time?"

"It'd feel better if we weren't being chased." She gave him a shaky smile and returned his squeeze. "But it's better than doing this alone. Thank you."

The drive back around the mountain took thirty minutes. York eyed his gas gauge. Half a tank. He chewed the inside of his lip. Could they risk a drive into town? No. They'd go farther and stop at a station down the freeway. They needed to be prepared for anything. And running out of gas wasn't an option.

His cell phone rang causing him to jerk the wheel and almost run them into the ditch. Caller ID showed Mrs. Olsen.

"Yes?"

"Don't stop in front of the house. Back up if you have to. Take the lake road. I know it's a bit of a drive, but there's been a car parked in front of the house for the last half hour. I've put the supplies in the old cotton shed."

"Thank you." *God, bless that woman. Protect*

*her from the danger I've put her in.*

"You can thank me by getting out of this alive." Click.

York cut the lights, stopped, and backed up. His heart almost stopped as he realized how close they'd come to being caught. He sped back the way they'd come, turned down a driveway to an empty house, stopped, and succumbed to the tension he'd been holding in for the last hour. His hands trembled. Nausea rose. He closed his eyes and let his forehead rest on the steering wheel.

*I'm a writer, Lord. Not a special agent. A father. Not a rough and tumble hunter.*

He took a deep breath and straightened. "Okay. I'm ready now. Just needed a break for a moment." He smiled at his passengers. "Ready for the next phase of this God-forsaken adventure?"

# CHAPTER NINETEEN

I f York lost his strength, what would they do?

Darcie bit her lip to keep the tears at bay. Fear, more raw than any she'd experienced before, rose and threatened to choke her. Her throat muscles burned. She wanted to get to the safety of the cabin. Now.

Then look for the package at first light. Anything to end this. Even if that meant turning over what they found to the police and letting the authorities take it from there.

York reached across her and yanked open the glove compartment. He tossed a black vinyl book in her lap. "Here's your battle guide. Read it. Starting with the book of Luke."

"You want me to read the Bible now?" He must be insane. When their lives were at stake?

"I'm *telling* you to read it. It's not a request." York slammed the gear shift into reverse and backed from the driveway, leaving the headlights off. "If you don't get on the same page, so to speak, as myself, I can't help you, and neither can God."

If he would have dumped a bucket of ice water on her head, she couldn't have been more shocked. Bullets flying past them, killers stalking them, and he wanted her to crack the pages of a book. Darcie shook her head. Fine. She'd read. As soon as she had light to read by. But that didn't mean she wanted anything to do with God.

York drove back the way they'd come, then pulled down a well-maintained dirt road before stopping behind a white-paneled house. "Y'all stay here. If I'm not back in five minutes, drive away. Anywhere. Or better yet, to the police station. Just keep my kids safe."

Darcie's breathing increased. Her heart pounded as he slunk away, keeping to the shadows. He turned toward her, the dark too deep for her to decipher his features. She glanced over her shoulders and noticed the children asleep in the back seat. She sighed. To be that secure. Something she hadn't had as a child. To trust completely the ability for someone to protect her. York would risk his life for his children. *Was* risking his life for her at that moment, and all she did was complain about her fear.

That knowledge raised emotions she'd never experienced before. A different kind of fear. One more for the safety of others, than herself. A small sense of safety. Darcie clutched the book in her hand. Was this what gave York his confidence?

She rubbed her fingers across the worn leather of

the Bible. Were the answers really between these pages? Her grandmother had thought so. York thought so.

Did they hold the key to true security? Peace?

One of the verses her grandmother used to recite came to mind. The dear woman said it each night as she tucked Darcie into bed. Even when Darcie claimed she was too old for bedtime riddles. *You will not be afraid when you lie down. When you lie down, your sleep will be sweet.* Slumber had never felt like that before then.

She peered through the night for York. How long had it been? She should've glanced at her watch when he left. She pressed the illumination button. Five after ten. She'd give him five more minutes, then get her and the kids away. But where would they go? They couldn't drive aimlessly, waiting for another knight in shining armor to put his life on hold and help them. What would she tell Sam and Sarah if their father didn't return?

Five minutes! What had he been thinking? It had to take longer than that to sneak around the house and grab the supplies. He'd probably have to make more than one trip, wouldn't he? He'd given Mrs. Olsen a long list.

Darcie banged her head against the back of the seat. Given more time, she probably could have come to care for the motherly old woman.

A twig snapped outside her window. She jerked upright. An animal? She narrowed her eyes and locked the door then smiled. The back window was busted out. Locking her door seemed a waste of time. A bush rustled, and Darcie released a sigh when a cat wandered into sight. "Almost gave me a heart attack."

Her whisper made the confines of the truck feel less lonely. Less dark. She almost wished one of the children would wake and keep her company, then chided herself for being foolish. "Sleep is their release." She reached over the seat and recited the same verse her grandmother used, laying a hand on each dark-haired head.

~

This was taking too long. York kept his back plastered against the house. The white paint on the cotton shed gleamed bright in the moonlight. Could he make it the fifty feet without being seen? Could he take the chance of *not* risking it? He shook his head. They needed the supplies in that building, and he'd already been gone longer than the five minutes. For the first time since he'd met her, he prayed Darcie wouldn't follow his order to leave him stranded.

As emotionally wounded as she was, she'd be in no shape to save Sam and Sarah. She would head straight for the police station. As much as he trusted Roger, York didn't believe the small town department could keep his family safe.

The burden on his shoulders lay heavy as the thick mud along the river bottom. He'd failed Michelle. He couldn't fail Darcie and the kids.

A small cluster of clouds floated in front of the moon. Thanking God for the cover, York darted to the shed. Unlocked. *Bless you, Mrs. Olsen.* He slid the well-oiled door open enough to squeeze through and tripped over a pile of stuff on the floor.

He sprawled across the concrete floor and choked back the sneeze that wanted to erupt with the dust. With the woman's obsession for cleanliness, this small amount of dirt was as foreign as if he suddenly found himself transported to a European city. Granted, her brother was a widower, but she'd cared for him the last few years. York crawled to the pile he'd tripped over.

His housekeeper outdid herself. Two boxes of food, four sleeping bags, a duffel bag, and a bulging black garbage bag lay right inside the door. York grabbed as much as he could carry then slipped back outside. Still partially obscured, the moon's beams cast more shadows, and York struggled with his heavy load back to the truck.

Darcie whipped around when he tossed the bags into the back. He approached her window. "Glad to see you didn't listen. I've one more load. Be right back. Give me fifteen minutes."

She nodded, her eyes large and shining through the dark. He smiled to see her clutching his Bible like a life-line. Only a matter of time, Lord. He dashed back to the shadows.

He rounded the corner of the house, and froze. A man leaned against the idling sedan. The crimson end of a burning cigarette shined like a beacon inside the car parked out front. "Quiet. I think I heard something." The standing man took a step toward the house.

York ducked back and melted against the siding of the Olsen home. He glanced upward. *I need another covering, Lord.*

"Go see what it is." The cigarette flicked onto the

street.

"It's just a cat. I saw one earlier. Stop being so nervous."

York slid along the wall of the house, knocking a tin bucket into a stack of firewood. He paused and held his breath.

"That wasn't no cat!" The men's voices floated on the evening breeze. Amplified in the country stillness.

"There're all kinds of critters out here. I told you we was wasting our time sitting in front of these old people's house. Only a fool would come back here."

Red and blue flashing lights stopped beside the parked sedan. Muted voices reached York's ears. Without a second thought he darted to the shed, grabbed what was left, and lumbered back to the waiting Darcie. He tossed the last of the supplies in the back, then joined Darcie in the truck, taking a minute to hunch in the seat and restore his racing heart to normal.

"What? Were you seen?" Darcie laid a hand on his arm. "What happened to you?"

"I tripped. I don't think anyone saw me. A police car stopped beside the men waiting out front. I'm sure it's the guys that have been following us. The cops are probably wondering why they're parked on the side of the highway." York turned the key in the ignition. "Hopefully, they'll detain the driver long enough for us to get away unseen." He steered the truck in a tight circle and eased forward.

Shots as rapid as popping corn splintered the dark. Darcie dropped the Bible and clapped her hands over her mouth. York pressed the gas and sped back down the dirt road. As they burst back onto the highway, he glanced over. The cruiser's lights still flashed.

"Who shot who?" Darcie asked.

"I'm guessing the bad guys got the good guys." *Please, don't let Roger have been on duty tonight, Lord.*

The sedan's lights brightened the highway behind them, and York continued to increase his speed. He didn't think the sedan could see him at this distance, but he still waited until the highway curved before flicking on his own lights. He hoped he'd left nothing behind to let their pursuers know he owned a hunting cabin. If they searched real estate titles, they'd discover the fact. He prayed they weren't that thorough.

He sighed, remembering the copy of the title in his desk drawer. He'd stashed it there when he'd considered selling the piece of land. How many more surprises lurked, waiting until he overcame one obstacle, only to be presented with another?

Few cars traveled after ten at night. York sped up and pulled in front of a motor home. The driver honked. York tossed a wave over his shoulder. The next exit loomed and he raced down it, leading them to an all-night convenience store that sold gas.

# CHAPTER TWENTY

U gh! The trucks headlight's spotlighted a cabin sporting warped wooden shingles, a lopsided porch, and missing steps. A place so familiar to her childhood home, Darcie's shoulders slumped. On the bright side, if anyone drove by, they'd think the place deserted.

"Let's get things unloaded then I'll pull the truck into the woods." York shoved a sleeping bag into her arms. "I know it doesn't look like much, but no one besides Mrs. Olsen knows we're here."

Darcie nodded. God couldn't find them in this place. Her first step sent her foot plunging through a dry-rotted slab of wood. She lifted her foot from the hole and proceeded with care to the porch. "Watch the stairs!" She wanted to cry. She'd lived in shabby places, but this one could grace the cover of Ramshackle Cabins of the South.

A strong shoulder shove against the door let her

enter a room clouded with dust motes and cobwebs. Darcie shuddered and looked for the cleanest dirt-covered surface on which to toss the sleeping bag. Sagging cots were placed around the perimeter of the room, and she tossed the bag on the nearest one.

A table built with two-by-fours took up precedence in the center of their new home. One wall housed a massive stone fireplace with the largest painting of a hunting scene she'd ever laid eyes on. The door to her left showed an out-of-date kitchen, with *thank you, God*, a stove and kerosene powered refrigerator. A broom sat propped in a corner.

With a full moon casting beams of white light through the grimy windows, the cabin had a haunted look. A place full of shadows.

No time like the present. Darcie lit a lantern, grabbed the broom, and feverishly sent waves of dirt billowing out the back door. York plopped the rest of the supplies on the dirty table and started to unload.

"Not until I've cleaned this place up." Darcie brandished the broom. "I can't live like this and neither should the kids."

York held up his hands. "Okay, fine. There's a well out back for water if you need it. I'll get out of your way and hide the truck."

Sam scooted in when York rushed back out. "What a dump."

Darcie sighed and handed him a stained plastic bucket. "Can you fill this at the well for me?"

"Better than sitting around here. There isn't even a TV." He stomped outside.

"Cool! Books." Sarah made a beeline for a wooden shelf above the fireplace. "Hardy boys?"

Darcie laughed at her disgusted expression. "They were probably your Dad's."

"Dad never came here. This belonged to Mom's family. My uncle died when he was younger. They're probably his." Sarah grabbed a book and plopped on the nearest cot, sending another wave of dust into the air. "My uncle shot himself."

"Before you get too comfortable, can you drag those cots outside? I need to beat the dirt out of them." Shot himself? Darcie shuddered.

An hour later, and having been avoided by the Wardell family because of her bossy attitude, Darcie studied the results of her hard labor. Rustic, but clean. She glanced at the ceiling. If it didn't rain. Then she'd have mud to deal with. She set to work unpacking the supplies, laying them out on the table. As if he knew when the cleaning frenzy was over, York reappeared by her side.

"A lantern, oil, kerosene, whistles, walky-talkies. Mrs. Olsen thought of things I didn't." York shook his head. "She's an amazing woman." He strode to the fireplace, moved the picture above it and revealed a safe. With a couple twirls of the dial, he opened it to reveal a shotgun and a box of shells. "Once I clean this, it ought to be as good as new."

"Plan on going hunting?" Darcie stacked the canned food in the single cabinet beside the sink. "Why's the gun in a safe? Seems like a strange place to store it."

"Protection. Less chance of accidents. Glass can be broken. Most locks can be cut. It's not really a safe. My father-in-law built it special for his guns after an unfortunate accident."

Darcie's mind seized on protection. That single word seized Darcie's heart in an iron fist. "You think they'll find us."

"Eventually. My name is on the deed. Find that, and they'll know we're here."

"Then we should have gone somewhere else!"

"There is nowhere else." York laid the gun and shells on the table. "We can't run aimlessly. We've got to find that package. What did Tony say, exactly?"

Darcie plopped in one of the four straight backed chairs. "He hid a package containing a list of names and a recorded tape. Supposedly, the names are of men laundering money and using it in a gambling ring. He caught one of their confessions on a hidden recorder. Besides that, he managed to say, 'that shack in Shadow Springs'." Darcie shrugged. "There's lots of them. I assumed maybe my mother's house, but I couldn't find a sign of it. My next stop was going to be my grandmother's old place."

"Okay. We go there tomorrow."

~

After a dinner of beans that Darcie overcooked and slathered with ketchup, York set to work cleaning the gun by the light of a kerosene lamp. He'd meant to install lighting in the cabin since the day he inherited it, but besides the gas to the stove, lanterns and the fireplace were the only sources of light. If they wanted the place to look uninhabited from the outside, lighting a fire was out.

Darcie sat staring at the closed Bible like the words inside would bite her. Sam and Sarah hunched over worn copies of Hardy Boy books. York smiled. At least the lack of electricity got Sam to open a book, even if forced to by boredom.

How long until they were found? York figured at least two days, hopefully longer. He racked his brain trying to come up with some way of rigging an alarm system around the perimeter of the cabin but feared that would alert the men they'd actually found an occupied building. He rubbed a grease cloth down the gun's barrel. Could he shoot them if the need arose? He'd never shot a man before. Only deer and rabbits for food.

This was ridiculous. They'd find that package and turn it over to the police first chance. Once the men were in custody, they could go home. Finished with the rifle, he laid it across the fireplace mantel. "Sam, if you so much as touch this rifle, you'll be sorry."

Sam glanced up from his book. "I'm a good shot, Dad."

"I know, but accidents happen. That's my final word. Don't touch it." York turned to Darcie. "Do you know how to shoot?"

"No. I've never held a gun."

"Are you going to read that Bible, or stare a hole through it?"

"Don't rush me." Her brows drew together in a frown.

"It's not that bad." He began unrolling the sleeping bags on top of the cots. "You'll be surprised at just how much it fits life today.

Timeless."

"Uh-huh." She opened to the index.

"Come on, guys." York pointed to the beds. "I'm turning off the lamp to save the oil, so that means bedtime. The sun rises early on the mountain."

Darcie sighed, smiled, and closed the Bible. "Guess I'll start reading tomorrow."

York grinned. "I'm almost tempted to leave the lamp burning just for you."

"But I'm really tired. Probably wouldn't remember a word I read." She moved to the cot beside Sarah and slipped between the layers of the bag. "Good night."

"Good night." York moved to the window and stared into the night.

Without street lamps, the dark was complete. His house grew dark at night, but up here, the shadows menaced, as if eager to reach beyond the log walls to the occupants. He shook off his thoughts. Writing books caused his imagination to work overtime. He glanced at his cell phone. Three bars. At least they got reception. A miracle in itself. He'd plug it into the car charger tomorrow.

Rechecking the sliding planks that locked the door from the inside, he moved back to the window. Fatigue settled on his shoulders as heavy as the humid air outside. He leaned his forehead against the cool glass. *Lord, help us in our search tomorrow. We need to end this soon.*

Would his children have been safer with Mrs. Olsen? Fear of them being used as bait made him disregard that idea. He'd keep them with him. Killers or not; he wanted to know where his children were at all times.

Then, there was Darcie. A beautiful sprite of a woman who drove him to distraction. He seemed to take two steps closer to her for every one step back. He found himself falling for the feisty widow in spite of his resolve to the contrary. A thought as dangerous as what waited for them in the night.

York laid on top of the bed left for him and used his folded arm as a pillow. Ironic, really, that what happened in his books was happening in his life. Almost as if his written words conjured the circumstances. He scoffed.

If life were fiction, there'd be no doubt of them getting away unharmed. After all, readers wanted a happy ending. The good guy always wins, and the boy gets the girl.

*Lord, let it be so.*

# CHAPTER TWENTY-ONE

T he Bible still sat where she'd left it the night before. The smooth leather cover screamed, "Pick me up!" Darcie wrinkled her nose and headed to the ancient kitchen to pour cereal for a modest breakfast. Snores emanated from York and snuffles from Sam, while Sarah slept as peaceful as a cherub.

She entertained the idea of them being her family. A pioneering family struggling to tame the land and make a name for themselves. She giggled.

"What's so funny?" York slid his legs over the side of his cot and sat up. Mahogany hair ruffled and sticking in all directions. He looked so much like his son, Darcie had to fight the urge to wrap him in her arms.

Her face heated. "Nothing." She turned to pour the milk.

York shook the children awake. "Come on, guys. We're going on a treasure hunt."

"Yippee!" Sam bolted from the bed. Sarah followed at a sleepier pace, rubbing the sleep from her eyes.

To the tune of happy slurping from Sam and Sarah, Darcie spooned cold cereal into her mouth. From the corner of her eyes, she snuck glances at York. Sporting a five-o'clock shadow the man looked good enough to eat. She mentally shook herself. Idiot! *You're in a fight for survival and you're comparing a man to food.*

Breakfast over and dishes stacked in the single-side stainless steel sink, the four of them piled back into the truck, fighting brambles to open the doors. York hung his rifle on a gun rack in the back and looked her way. "Where to first?"

"My grandmother's, I guess. I've already checked the house and barn at my mother's. I also checked my old tree house for good measure."

"Any other buildings on the property?"

"A well house."

York chewed the inside of his cheek. "I don't imagine anything could be hidden there. Your grandmother's place isn't really a shack, though. I did some handy-man jobs for her before she died."

Darcie remembered the cutting remarks Tony made about the two-bedroom home. "In Tony's eyes it was." Had he actually said in the shack, or was that the general location? He'd been so difficult to understand through the bubbles of blood welling in his mouth from internal injuries. What if she led them all on a wild goose chase?

Maybe Tony had been delirious. She laid her head sideways, resting it on the window.

York drove a round-about way and pulled behind the small cabin with peeling blue paint. Darcie's heart lurched. Her only happy childhood days had been spent within these four walls. She supposed the house belonged to her now. Once everything was settled, she'd check with her grandmother's lawyer in Little Rock. No reason to let anyone else know she'd returned.

To the east sat a storage shed. Behind the house a dry well, covered with a rotting plank of wood, and a dog house. Not a lot of places to search. York sent the children around back.

"What are we looking for?" Sam asked.

"Anything that looks like it doesn't belong where ever you find it."

"Gee, thanks, Dad. That tells me a lot."

York gave his son a swat on the bottom then pulled a whistle from his jeans pocket. "Wear this and go have fun." He turned to Darcie. "Shall we start with the house?"

York jimmied the lock on the front door and stepped aside to let Darcie enter first. Memories assaulted her so strong she thought she could smell her grandmother's pineapple upside down cake. She swallowed the urge to call out her name and blinked back tears.

Leaving York in the living room, she moved to the miniscule kitchen. Her grandmother stood at the kitchen sink elbow deep in fragrant suds. She turned with a smile.

"Hey, Darcie!" York's voice cut through the reminiscing. "I'm going to go through this pile of books."

"Okay." Darcie wiped her eyes on her sleeve. She'd start with the cabinets. Someone had already cleaned out most everything. Vandals, maybe? Squatters? She shook her head. At least they hadn't trashed the place. Grandma would've said, "If they need it bad enough to steal, they can have it."

After checking empty cupboards, Darcie stood in the middle of the room and turned in a slow circle, scanning for any hiding places. She pulled up a chair and looked in the cabinet above the refrigerator. Empty. She moved to the bathroom. The room not much bigger than a closet held only a toilet, pedestal sink, and a shower. Her gaze moved over the floor and walls, checking for loose tiles. Nothing.

York appeared behind her and Darcie whirled. "You scared me."

"Sorry. Find anything?"

"Nothing. I don't think it's in the house." He stood too close for comfort and she stepped back.

"I agree. Let's move outside. Maybe the kids found something."

"Maybe it isn't here. It could be at my mother's. Or Tony's parents." Darcie squeezed past him. "Only problem with that is, they still live there." And they didn't like her. Detested her and blamed her for their son's death.

~

York watched Darcie as she stepped outside. Had she seen his feelings reflected in his eyes? He'd wanted to wrap his arms around her and banish the cloud of melancholy that threatened to crush her. He should've come here alone. Being back after her grandmother's death was too much. Going to her in-law's would be tougher. He'd heard about the Thayer's feelings for their daughter-in-law. How she'd corrupted their son.

He shook his head. Blind to their son's faults, they'd shifted blame to Darcie. They had no other option. They had to rule out every possible hiding place. Tomorrow, they'd go to the Thayer's home, regardless of the reception they would receive.

York would like to see some of the fire he'd witnessed when he'd first found Darcie. Most of the time recently, she resembled a beaten puppy. Where was the spark that went with the red hair?

By the time he stepped into the afternoon sunlight, Darcie already rummaged around in the storage shed, tossing out farming tools and bags of moldy birdseed. York glanced around for Sam and Sarah. They poked sticks into a hole in the house's foundation. Sam yelled out they'd found a corn snake. York waved an acknowledgement and joined Darcie inside the shed.

Tears left tracks in the dirt on her face. York squatted beside her. "Are you all right?"

She lifted her face to him. "I never had a chance to say goodbye. She died while I was in the hospital recovering from the accident."

"How can I help?" Her devastated expression cut at his heart.

"Could you hold me?"

York sat cross-legged on the concrete floor and cradled her in his lap like he did Sarah when she was upset. Except Darcie felt completely different. Soft and all woman. Her hair smelled of the strawberry shampoo she used. Sobs shook her body, and his tee-shirt beneath her cheek grew damp.

"I'm sorry." Darcie pulled back and sniffed. "It's a bit much, you know? The running, her death, everything. And, I have to admit to some guilt over dragging you and the kids into this. I really thought I could get a job and find the package in a short amount of time. Those men caught up to me faster than I expected.

"When I was married to Tony, I didn't tell anyone where we were from. He said he had a reputation to uphold and didn't want anyone to know we came from a hick town in upper Arkansas." She locked gazes with him, her own emerald, overflowing pools. "How did they know?"

York shrugged. "It's not that difficult to find out about someone. Not if you know where to look."

"Right." She stood. "I have this horrible feeling that time is running out. The only reason I'm still alive is that they want that package and expect me to know where it is. I don't! Why would Tony hide something where it would be difficult for me to find it?"

"I doubt he expected to die before retrieving it." He pushed to his feet. "We'll find it."

"Well, it ain't here." Darcie brushed off her shorts. "Which means I've got to do what I'd been putting off and said I would never do again. Visit Tony's parents. He might have told them something. Do you think we could sneak?"

York laughed. "I think it's best if we ask them outright. Maybe he gave it to them or put it in a safety deposit box and they have the key."

Darcie's shoulders slumped. "I should've checked with them first. It won't be pleasant though."

"Don't beat yourself--"

Sarah screamed.

# CHAPTER TWENTY-TWO

York bolted to his feet then sprinted around the corner of the house.

Sam dangled the corn snake over Sarah's head. She cowered, hands covering her hand. "Sam! You scared me to death. Stop right this instant."

"I'm just playing." Sam stuffed the snake in his pocket. "I can't help it if Sarah's a baby."

"Put the snake back where you found it." York took a deep breath to steady his nerves. His hands shook. His heart pounded.

What would he have done if he'd found his children being held hostage by two gunmen? Resolving not to leave the gun out of reach again, he marched to retrieve it from the gun rack in the truck.

His knees buckled and he leaned against the bumper. A hero from one of his novels, he wasn't. *Lord, what am I doing here*? He dug his cell phone from his pocket and punched in Roger's number. While it rang on the other end, he marched back to the house.

Darcie knelt beside Sarah and wiped away her tears. A grin split the pretty freckled face. York shook his head. Of course she would think terrorizing someone with a reptile would be funny. He smiled, remembering the tomboy he'd observed from a distance during high school.

"This is Roger."

"It's York."

"Know anything about my men getting shot last night?"

York sagged against the wall. Roger never had been one to mince words. "I was at the Olsen place getting supplies. A dark-colored sedan was parked out front. The cruiser pulled up, I took advantage of the distraction, and we split. I'm glad it wasn't you, Roger."

"Yeah, me too. There's no keeping me out of this now, York." The man sighed. "Where are you?"

"I'd rather not say. I doubt we'll be here longer than a day or two anyway."

"I could always trace the cell phone, York."

York ran his fingers through his hair. "I'll check in every morning by ten. If you don't hear from me, do that. If we run into trouble in the meantime, I'll call. Do you know whether the Thayer's are in town?"

"Last I heard they were. Just got back from a cruise. Why? You plan on paying them a visit?"

"Darcie thinks maybe Tony told them something about this mysterious package."

"Can't hurt, I guess. If you would tell me more, we could be looking on our end."

How much information would be too much? "I'm afraid if Darcie doesn't find it, the men won't stop."

"They won't either way. They aren't going to let that woman, or any of you, live. You know it, and I know it. The safest place is here in protective custody."

"Maybe." Footsteps pounded on the back porch. "Gotta go. I'll call you tomorrow." York pushed the end button and shoved the phone back in his pocket.

By the way Sam kept his hand moving around in his pocket, York knew the snake still resided in its new denim home. Darcie raised her eyebrows and shook her head. Fine. The snake could stay. Sam would have little else to keep him occupied while they went on a wild goose chase.

York grabbed the rifle from the cot. "Let's go. Daylight's wasting. Darcie, I put the Bible in the glove compartment for you."

Her mouth fell open then snapped shut. "I can't read in the truck. I get carsick."

"I'll drive slow."

"Why is this so important to you?"

"Kids, go wait in the truck. Honk the horn if you see anything." York waited until he and Darcie faced each other alone. "What if you don't make it through this alive? Have you thought of that? I can't, with any measure of being a good man, let you die without the reassurance of heaven."

"Good grief. I never said I wasn't saved. I just happen to believe God doesn't have time for me right now. And, to be honest, I have every right to be angry with him."

"Read the book of Matthew instead. Start with verse 7:25. It's about the birds and the lilies." He turned and stormed out of the cabin.

~

Birds and lilies? The man's insane.

Darcie tucked the Bible under her arm and climbed into the truck. What was his all-fired hurry? She'd accepted the Lord during a revival. She also knew you couldn't lose your salvation. What did it matter to him what her relationship with God was like?

There were more important things to worry about. Like staying alive.

Darcie paused. A year ago, staying alive wouldn't have mattered. Her entire existence had stemmed on fulfilling a promise that never should have been made. Now…She turned in her seat to look at the Wardells. Three heads stared her way. Life offered her another chance at what she'd lost. She glanced at the blue sky above the towering oak and pine trees.

For the first time since her brother's death, Darcie felt stirrings of forgiveness toward an almighty God who had a plan. He'd saved her brother from an unhappy childhood by calling him home at such a young age. Her husband, Tony's death, was a result of his own actions and choices. And Grandma, she'd had her eye on heaven for a long time.

"Are you ready?" York frowned.

*I'll try to follow your lead, Lord. You've got my*

*attention. But I'm not promising I won't have questions or doubts.* Darcie grinned. "Let's go."

"Are you okay?"

"Never better." Darcie opened the Bible to Matthew and read about not worrying. She was reminded of her worth. More than the birds of the air or the lilies of the fields. She continued with forgiveness and prayer. Peace settled over her despite their destination, slowing her racing heart.

By the time they pulled into the Thayers' driveway, strength flowed through her for the first time in many years. She took a deep breath and glanced toward the house.

Marsha Thayer, tall and thin as a reed, stepped onto the porch of a ranch-style house before York cut the engine. Her husband, rounder, but just as tall, joined her.

Darcie took a deep breath and shoved open her door.

York grasped her elbow. "Do you need me to go with you?"

"I'll be all right." It surprised her to realize she meant the words.

Her feet crunched across gravel as she made her way to the stoic pair. Marsha crossed her arms and glared. Anthony Thayer dropped into a rocking chair and covered his eyes with a beefy hand.

"Hello, Marsha. Anthony." Darcie squared her shoulders.

"What are you doing here?" Marsha's shrill voice rang across the yard. "I can not believe you would have the nerve to set foot on our property. After what you did."

"I know I'm the last person you want to set eyes on, but Tony's last words asked me to retrieve something, and I haven't been able to locate it. Did he by any chance leave anything here?"

"What makes you think we'd give you anything our dear son left?"

Dear son? Darcie couldn't count on both hands how many times Tony's parents had said he'd be the death of them. "Please. It's important."

Anthony spoke from beneath his hand. "He called the night before he died. Started to say he'd hidden something, but hung up before he could tell us what."

Darcie's heart sank. Her shoulders slumped. Coming had been a waste of time. "I'm sorry to have bothered you."

"Looks like you've moved on. That's York Wardell, the fancy writer, ain't it?" Marsha lifted her nose. "I've heard all about the two of you. Living under the same roof. Not married. You're just like your mother."

"I'm the children's nanny. Nothing more."

"And I'm the blessed Mary."

"Believe what you want, Marsha." Darcie studied the woman's weary face. She'd aged since the last time she'd seen her almost two years ago. "I really am sorry about Tony. You lost a son. I lost a husband and a child."

"You were pregnant?"

Darcie nodded and blinked back tears.

Marsha sagged into the rocker beside her husband. "Tony never told us. A grandchild. Oh, how much we've lost." She covered her face with her hands and sobbed.

Anthony placed a hand on her shoulder. "There's a lot our son didn't tell us." He raised red-rimmed eyes to Darcie. "There were men here looking for you this morning. I told them we haven't seen you in almost two years. I don't think they were friends. What did my son do?"

Darcie didn't want to tell them. She saw no need to sully their view of Tony. An only child, he'd been raised spoiled and self-centered. Something she hadn't seen until too late. "Nothing. I don't know who would be looking for me."

"Don't lie. Are you in trouble with the law?"

"No." Darcie looked toward the truck, silently pleading for York to rescue her. "Why would you ask that?"

"Because I caught a glimpse of a gun under one of the men's jacket." Anthony rose and towered over Darcie. She stepped back and heard York open the truck door. "Marsha may not believe it, but I knew about my son's gambling habit. Looks to me like he died and left you holding the bag."

Had everyone know about Tony's gambling but her? Had she known the man she'd married at all? "He told me he hid a package in a shack. I was hoping he'd said something to you."

Anthony shook his head. "Not a thing. But my guess is y'all need to get going. Those men will be back. And, this time, I can't honestly say you weren't here." He stepped back to his wife's side. "We won't be either. Marsha, pack a bag. We're visiting your sister." He reached into his pocket and tossed Darcie a key. "There's an old hunting cabin about a half an hour drive from here. Up Elk road. Turn right at a red mailbox. Bet whatever he hid is there. I'd planned on going there later today to check on its upkeep."

Darcie caught the key and stared. "Anyone else know where the cabin is?"

"It's common knowledge around these parts. We've always kept an open door policy on that cabin."

# CHAPTER TWENTY-THREE

York leaned against the hood of the Ford. "What's that?"

"A key." Darcie bounced it in her hand.

"So, Tony did tell them where it is."

"I wish." Darcie raised her head and grinned. "But it's to another hunting cabin. One that belongs to the Thayers. We're one step closer. I can feel it." Hope leaped in her chest only to die when she remembered Anthony's words of caution. "Those two men were here earlier asking about me and Tony."

York opened his door and slid behind the wheel. He turned when Darcie settled in her seat. "Let's give the key to Roger."

She snapped her head up. "Why? We can do this."

"At what expense?" He motioned toward the back seat.

Darcie's breath hitched. "You're right. This scares me to death. I've never relied on the police before. What if they can't find it?"

"We'll keep looking too." York turned the key in the ignition. "I think it's best we have the law on our side. I'd feel a lot safer digging around with a couple of armed officers next to me."

"Okay." Darcie transferred her attention out the window. Cops. They'd never helped her before. Numerous child abuse complaints had been turned in by teachers and neighbors, depicting Darcie's mother as the neglectful parent she'd been. Nothing had happened. At least not until her brother Davie's death. She shrugged. York seemed confident in his friend Roger. Maybe things would be all right.

Her eyes stung with unshed tears. Hours before she'd been hopeful with a promise to rely on God. Now, she'd practically tossed that concept out the window. Trusting wouldn't come easy. With God or anyone else. She'd relied on one person, her grandmother, and she resided in heaven. Darcie wanted to trust York but feared he'd break her heart easier than their pursuers could end her life.

She focused on the verse about God caring for the sparrows. Something else nagged at her mind. Words her grandmother told her years ago. Jesus had called Davie home. Now he rested in loving arms, never to cry or hurt again. Darcie's tears dried. Grandma held her sweet grandson with Jesus watching. Why had Darcie forgotten those words of comfort? She'd spent so many useless years bitter and aching.

"York?"

"Yes?"

"I've been thinking about what I've read, and remembering things I'd heard in the past. I can't help but wonder why this is happening?" Darcie faced him. "I'm trying to trust, I really am."

"I think it's happening so you can put these guys away."

"That idea is so simple."

"It often is." York pulled into the police station parking lot and cut the engine. "That's why it's so hard to comprehend. Since God is mighty, we tend to think his plans have to be complex."

"It's hard to wrap my brain around."

York laughed. "That, too, is common. Just accept the gift, Darcie. God is in control. Not always the way we'd like, but He is."

Darcie shoved open her door and pulled the seat forward so Sam and Sarah could climb out of the truck. York's words were the understatement of the year.

~

Roger twirled an ink pen while Darcie recited how she'd ended up in the predicament she was in. Even hearing it again, York found it difficult to believe. And he'd been living it! The only shining spot in the whole horrifying fiasco was Darcie's growing renewal in her faith.

York glanced to where his children played Go Fish with the police station's receptionist. He wanted life to go back to normal. They should enjoy their summer vacation. Not be running from gun men.

"Well." Roger dropped the pen on his desk.

"That's some story. Why didn't you come to me sooner?"

Darcie's face reddened. "I, um…"

"Don't trust the police." Roger leaned forward and folded his hands. "I know your background. I also know your late husband's." He shoved a folder toward her. "He's got a rap sheet a mile long."

"I didn't know." Darcie raised her wide-eyed gaze to York's. "I promise."

More secrets. York's heart sank. "What kind of crimes? Why do you have a file on Tony? "

"Robbery, car theft, petty assault. We've had the list a while. Seems a robbery that occurred over a year ago had Tony's fingerprints at the scene. We've been keeping an eye out for him." Roger leaned back in his chair. "His crimes started right out of high school. *Your* record, Mrs. Thayer, is clean, despite your marriage to the man. How did you manage that?"

Darcie's cheeks reddened. She folded her hands tight enough together to turn her knuckles white. "Tony was gone a lot. On business, he said. Until the night he died, when he filled me in on some of his dealings, I thought he was a salesman." She bowed her head and dug the cabin key out of her pocket.

"Tony's parents gave me this. Said maybe he hid the package at their cabin." She tossed the key onto the desk. "I don't want anything more to do with it."

"At least he kept you out of his crime." York shoved his chair back and paced. He shoved his fingers through his hair. From the surprised look on Darcie's face, she'd been as unaware of Tony's list of crimes as he had. Regardless of the fact, York wanted to shake her and find out what other information she might be hiding.

"We'll go by the cabin tomorrow." Roger speared York with a gaze. "None of you disappear. I want to be able to get a hold of you at a moment's notice." He switched to Darcie. "I also expect you with us when we search. Tomorrow morning, eight a.m., the Thayer cabin. I've got to go to the hospital to check on my men. Thankfully, they weren't killed. York, stay a minute, please."

Darcie rose and avoided his eyes. She scuttled past him and joined the children in the front of the building. At Roger's wave, York resumed his seat and waited for the other man to speak.

Roger folded his arms behind his head and leaned back in his chair. "Well?"

"What?"

"Do you think she's as innocent as she looks?"

York squared his chin. "Yes. I don't think she knew what her husband was involved in. He told her he had gambling debts and owed a loan shark a lot of money."

"That's true. He owes about fifty thousand dollars."

York thought he'd lose his lunch. "And now they want Darcie to pay it?"

"I don't know." Roger shrugged. "They definitely don't seem to want her to find that list. I shouldn't be telling you all this, but we've known each other for a long time. I think you should be aware of what's going on. Richard Leroy," He slid a photo to York.

"Is one really bad guy. We've had our eye on him for some time. One of his men turned, providing us with sketchy information. He was found shot to death a few days after he squealed. If we can put Leroy away, Darcie will be safe, along with a lot of other people." Roger leaned back in his chair. "The body you brought me is another petty criminal. Probably one of Leroy's men."

York picked up the 8 x 10 photocopy. A balding middle-aged man stared back in black and white. "Not someone you'd notice on the street."

"That's what makes him so difficult to catch. Hires dummies to do his work then sits back and reaps the profits." Roger let his chair fall back to the floor. "I want y'all back at your place."

"I'm not letting you use Darcie as bait." The guy was crazy. Certifiably insane. York shook his head. "Absolutely not."

"Don't let another pretty face blind you to the facts."

"What does that mean?" Blood pressure rising, York bolted to his feet.

"Settle down. You know I'm right. I warned you about Michelle, now I'm warning you about Darcie."

"They aren't the same." York clenched his fists. "And this time we're also placing my children in danger. Have you forgotten that?"

"Are you going to hit me over this? We've been friends for a long time. You have to trust me."

"Not at Darcie's expense."

"If we don't catch Leroy, then his crimes will continue. Suzy will have died in vain."

"Don't try laying the guilt trip on me. Suzy's death was unfortunate. A case of mistaken identity." York resumed his pacing, his heart racing faster than his moving feet. It could have been Darcie dead in Suzy's guesthouse. He drew a stuttering breath sharply through his nostrils. Keep it together. Falling apart won't help anyone.

"My two officers are in the hospital with gunshot wounds. One is critical." Roger rose and leaned forward, palms flat on his desk. "I want this to end."

York paused his furious marching. "So do I."

"Then let's do this."

York glanced to where Darcie stared at him through the glass partition dividing Roger's office from the reception area. He felt the blood drain from his face. He hadn't heard her approach. Her pale face told him she'd heard everything. Slowly, she nodded. York's stomach plummeted. Why hadn't he closed the door when she'd left? He was in danger of losing another woman he cared about.

She marched to his side, shoulders back, head high. "I'll do it."

"Darcie, no." York gripped her arm.

Tears welled in her eyes. "It's the only way. No more hiding. No more running. We go on with our lives, helping Roger to the best of our ability. If I die, then it's my time. I'm not afraid anymore."

*What about me? What about my feelings if you die or get hurt?* York shook off his selfish thoughts. *God, can't we come up with another plan?* He wrapped his arms around the woman whose head barely reached his chin. So small, so frail.

Closing his eyes, he rested his chin on top of her

head and met Roger's satisfied smile. "You'd better have someone watching the entire time, Roger. If not, be prepared to throw me in jail for assault, because I will hold you personally responsible."

# CHAPTER TWENTY-FOUR

Darcie covered her mouth and gasped. They'd been found. Again. She shook her head. Had they even been hidden? Would they ever get more than one step ahead of their pursuers? "How did they find us?"

"Obviously one of their contacts has access to county records. The cabin's in my name."

Their supplies lay strewn across the porch of the cabin. Smoke and flames towered through a hole in the shingle roof. Sam reached over her shoulder and locked the vehicle door.

Darcie reached to unlock the door. "We should at least salvage what we can. Why burn the place down?"

"One less place for us to hide. I'm much more inclined to follow my son's lead. Good job, Sam. Quick thinking on locking the door." A slow smile spread across York's face, and he turned back to Darcie. "What if they come back? I vote we leave." He pulled his cell phone from his pocket, called to report the fire, then turned the Ford toward home.

Home. The word warmed Darcie's soul despite the dangers that lurked out there in the open. York reached across and took her hand. His large hand engulfed her small one. The palm of his smoother than hers. The hands of a writer, not a laborer. His fingers strong. Safe.

"Ready to do this?"

"No." Darcie traced his knuckles with her finger. Pale scars dotted the surface. Marks of fighting when he was younger? York didn't seem the type. "But it must be done."

York squeezed. "Together?"

She nodded. "Together."

Pulling her hand free in order for York to concentrate driving on the curvy mountain road, Darcie stared into the darkening afternoon. Were they watching? She caught the rifle's reflection in the window. She had no doubt York would have to remove the weapon from the rack and fire at someone. Could he kill them? Could *she*? If it meant protecting York or the children—yes.

Before she realized it, they were home. Darcie shook Sam awake, and York gathered a sleeping Sarah in one arm and the rifle in the other. She waited a moment while the others went into the house.

A beautiful log cabin, designed for comfort and elegance. Not a fortress to hide from murderers. Her gaze slid in the direction of York's former home. Nature had almost overtaken the cement foundation, placing a layer of dirt and grass over most of it. *Please God, don't let things end up as in the past. No more death and destruction. No more shattered families. Not because of me.*

Prayer felt strange to her lips. Like the words left her mouth and got no farther than the tree tops. She glanced upward. Was God there? Would He listen to the pleas of a girl from the wrong side of the tracks? Grandma said he would. York believed so too.

As if her thoughts conjured him, York appeared in the doorway and raised an eyebrow at her then motioned his head toward the house. Obviously he wanted her to go first. She peered around her, noting the seclusion of the place and increased her pace into the house, flinching at the sound of the dead bolt as he latched it behind her. The rifle lay across the fireplace mantel, stark in its reality.

"You shouldn't be outside alone," York told her. "I'll put the kids to bed."

Darcie nodded and parted the curtains on the front window. Fading, summer sunlight flooded the yard, streaming through the glass and illuminating the varnished wood beneath her feet. God's creation at its finest. Yet they were locked behind log walls.

"I'm not sure they'll stay asleep. Daytime and sleep mean naps in my kids' minds. Something they swear they're too old for." Darcie heard York stomping down the stairs. "Don't stand by the window."

"You really think they want to kill me?" Darcie glanced over her shoulder. "I'm not the only one who knows about the package now. There's you and Roger."

York plopped onto the sofa. "They didn't have any qualms about murdering Suzy. I'm sure they won't think twice about the rest of us either."

Darcie let the drapes fall into place and turned. Her shoulders tensed in anticipation of a bullet. The inactivity would drive her crazy. The walls closed in, casting shadows in the corners. She trembled and folded her fists. Her nails dug into her palms. No fear, no fear. She'd promised God to trust.

Drawing in a shaky breath, she turned to York. "Are you hungry? I could fix some sandwiches."

"Come here." York patted the cushion next to him.

She shook her head.

"Why not?"

"I'll not crack under the pressure. I've survived for a year. There's no need to baby me."

"I'm not." He crooked his finger at her.

"I need to do something. Anything other than sitting, and waiting. Waiting for someone to bang down the front door." She waved an arm around the room. "We're hiding in a pile of wood. Do you know how fast this place would go up if torched? These log walls might stop a bullet, but they won't stand a chance against fire."

"Okay." He rose. "Come with me to check windows and doors. I want all the shutters closed." York stepped beside her and placed his lips next to her ear. "But I had something planned that would definitely take your mind off things."

Her skin tingled. Tears blurred her vision. York's arms were a safe haven, blocking out the horrors of the world. She breathed in the musky scent of him, a clean pine-smelling cologne.

She shook her head to clear it. How could York

think that way under the circumstances? Even as she drew away, Darcie thought of how nice his kiss would be.

~

She'd trembled at his words. He affected her. Why did she keep him at arm's length? Why not accept the help and love he offered? Her comment about the house going up in flames gripped his heart in a fiery fist. His mind raced, searching for an escape route if the need arose. The basement. They'd fit through one of the windows easily.

"We'll start downstairs." He took her hand in his.

Darcie jerked free of his hold at the top of the basement stairs. "I'll wait here."

"I need to show you what to do if you and the kids need to get out fast." He ran his gaze over her pale face.

"I don't like dark places."

"I'll be beside you the entire time." He held out his hand.

"My mother used to lock me in the tool shed when she had visitors." Darcie's eyes shimmered. "Sometimes she'd forget about me for hours." Her words choked off. "She usually left Davey in his crib."

"There's a light down here. You won't be alone. I'm right beside you." York wiggled his fingers. "Let me show you the dark isn't always something to be feared."

She nodded and stretched out her hand. York pulled her close. Shivers ran through her into her fingers, and he squeezed. Step-by-slow-step, they traversed their way down the ten stairs, York tugging Darcie behind him. He pulled a chain over their heads casting the dirt-floored room in weak light and tried visualizing the room through the eyes of someone afraid.

Dark corners loomed. Cobwebs decorated the few lit areas. Dusty cardboard cartons lay piled like discards. Not a room to instill comfort.

"There're plenty of places to hide down here. Behind the furnace. By that stack of boxes, but what I want you to do, is get through the window." He pointed to a rectangular square of light above a trunk. "You just lift the latch and push it open. This side of the basement faces the trees. Get out and run. Anywhere."

"Okay."

"I mean it. At any sign of danger. A stranger at the door, a whiff of smoke, a threatening phone call; you and the kids are out of here."

She frowned up at him. "What about you?"

"I'll be right behind you."

"After you provide a distraction."

York gripped her shoulders. "You and the kids are what matters to me."

"York—"

"Just do as I ask. Please."

"Okay." Her whispered response fell like ashes at his feet. Tears welled in emerald eyes. "I'll get the kids to safety." She lifted her chin. "Then I'll be back for you."

York laughed. "You've got spirit. Chances are, you won't need to fulfill that promise. I don't intend to be left behind if the need to run presents itself. Are we done here?"

"More than." Darcie almost sprinted up the stairs. Still grinning, York followed.

Sam stood in the kitchen, hair tousled from his brief nap. "What are y'all doing down there?"

York clapped him on the shoulder. "Just looking around. Showing Darcie parts of the house she hasn't seen."

"Isn't the basement great?" Sam opened the refrigerator. "It makes a wonderful fort or hide 'n go seek place. Sarah won't go down there. But I love it." He held up a soda. York nodded.

The difference between Darcie's childhood and the way his kids had been raised wasn't lost on him. Sam and Sarah had known loving discipline their entire lives. Darcie had only neglect and abuse until a teenager. York's heart ached. No child should live as she'd done. No young girl should hold her baby brother as he died in her arms. Yet, despite it all, she showed a tough resilience. York vowed to make her life better. After they put all this madness behind them.

Someone pounded on the front door. He whirled. "Get Sarah. Then the three of you wait in the kitchen. Anything seems remotely dangerous, you leave."

Darcie dashed out of the room. Her steps thundered as she charged up the stairs.

"Dad?" Sam's eyes grew wide. The door banged again. Sam's can of open soda fell with a splash to the tiled kitchen floor.

"Stay here, Sam." York grabbed the rifle from the mantel and parted the curtains beside the door.

# CHAPTER TWENTY-FIVE

Mrs. Olsen stood on the porch, arms loaded with grocery bags, casting glances over her shoulder. She raised a foot to kick at the door again, and York opened it. "Mrs. Olsen. What are you doing here?"

"So it's true." She shoved past him. "Y'all came down from the cabin and holed up here." She deposited the bags on the kitchen table. "When I heard the cabin burned, I suspected you'd come back."

"Roger told us—" Darcie's appearance with a sleepy Sarah distracted York from his explanation. "It's all right, Darcie." She laid Sarah on the sofa.

"Roger is using that girl as bait, ain't he?" Mrs. Olsen set her lips in a firm line. "I always said he didn't have the sense God gave a goose." She started unloading groceries and placed a gallon of milk in the refrigerator. "Guess he's better than nothing though."

"You shouldn't be here." York stilled the woman's busy hands. "It isn't safe. And what makes you think Roger is using Darcie?"

"If it's safe enough for you and the children, it's safe enough for me." She lifted her chin. "Guess you heard about the officers shot outside my house? I stormed into the police station wanting to know what's what. I gleaned enough information from Roger to put the pieces together myself."

"I saw the officers." *I was there.*

"Well, then you know this isn't one of your books." Mrs. Olsen set fists on her plump hips. "You can't write the ending to your satisfaction. Real life doesn't always end the way you'd like."

York ran a hand through his hair. "I know that. We're safe enough here. I've got the rifle loaded and another one upstairs. No one can break in without me knowing."

"Famous last words." She glanced around the room. "You've got food enough. Cell phone in case the land line gets cut. Is the truck full of gas? I can take it into town if you'd like. Have it back in half an hour."

"It's almost full but that would be great." The woman's generosity caused a lump to rise in York's throat. "You could be in danger by helping us."

"Who'd want to hurt me? I'm just hired help." She waggled her fingers, and York dug the Ford's keys from his pocket and dropped them in her hand.

York wrapped his arms around the woman and pulled her close. "You are the best."

She patted his back. "I know. Take care of that pretty girl and the young 'uns. I'll be right back."

She rushed out the front door, and York locked it behind her. When he turned, Darcie stood before him, tears in her eyes.

"I didn't think she liked me."

"Why would you think that?"

Darcie shrugged. "I guess I'm just not a very good judge of character. Look who I was married to."

"Oh, Darcie. I made my own marital mistake, but God blessed me with two beautiful children. Speaking of, I'd better see where they are." York checked on Sam's whereabouts and found him stuffing his face with cookies from one of the bags. Sarah dug through the refrigerator. York smiled, then led Darcie to the loveseat. "Mrs. Olsen thinks of me as a son. She's bossy, but loving and kind. She'll rake any woman who comes around me over the coals." Placing a finger beneath Darcie's chin, he lifted her face to his. "Don't beat yourself up over Tony. People aren't always what they seem. And I won't beat myself up anymore over Michelle, either."

"That's an idea."

York laughed. "Thanks a lot." When had he ever seen an opportunity to laugh at his wife's infidelity? The thought was ludicrous yet he couldn't help himself.

Darcie crossed her arms and plopped back against the cushions. "What really bothers me is, I'm not sure how much I really loved Tony. He was a means to getting me out of Shadow Springs. Don't get me wrong, I cared for him, but not like I…well, anyway."

York's heart leaped. What had she been going to say? That she cared for him? Could she finally have feelings for him that matched his for her?

~

What a dunce! After York kissed her forehead and went to save what was left of the cookies from Sam, Darcie slapped her forehead. The prime opportunity to state her feelings and she'd blown it. Maybe the timing was wrong. Staying alive should take precedence over declarations of love, right?

York's Bible stared at her from the coffee table. The sight didn't strike fear as it once had and she reached for it, letting the pages flutter open. The book opened to 1 Peter chapter three. One verse jumped off the page. *Who will hurt you if you do what is right?*

What is right? Going to the police? Loving York and his children? The only thing she knew with certainty was the men following them must be stopped. Fine. She'd put herself out there and trust in the God who wouldn't leave her alone. She prayed no one would have to pay for her past mistakes with their life.

She continued to flip through the pages, reading random verses. Verses of love, salvation, redemption, and trust.

God's words set roots in her heart, thrusting through the rocky crevices, providing life to Darcie's soul. Wings to her spirit. She said she'd follow his will, but giving up years of trusting no one would take time. She'd heard of instantaneous moments of acceptance, but that wasn't her style.

She glanced to where York laughed with Sam.

Then she switched her gaze to Sarah who moved to the sofa. The little girl's head bobbed with oncoming slumber. No sunlight broke through the cracks in the window curtains. Night fell outside as morning rose in her spirit. For the first time in a long time, Darcie relished a feeling of safety. Of love. Of family. Tears welled and coursed down her cheeks. *Please, God. Don't take it away, now that I've found what I've been looking for.*

Car tires crunched gravel outside. Darcie dried her eyes and peeked out. Mrs. Olsen emerged from York's truck and trotted to the porch. Darcie held the door open for her, quickly closing it behind the woman.

Mrs. Olsen patted her cheek. "Been crying, sweetie?" She looked at the book in Darcie's hand. "Oh, I see. I'm very happy for you. Choosing God is a life-changing decision." Leaving Darcie standing with her mouth open, the housekeeper breezed past her and to York's side.

"Here're your keys. I was tempted to stop by the station and give Roger a piece of my mind, but I restrained myself." Mrs. Olsen waved a hand toward the refrigerator. "There's plenty of food for as long as we hole up here. I didn't see any strangers in town, but now that folks are on the look-out, I doubt they'll be showing their faces."

York frowned. "What do you mean?"

Darcie moved closer in order to hear the conversation better.

"I mean, I put the word out. Tell just one or two people with loose lips, and the whole town will know that strangers are looking for y'all."

Darcie's heart plummeted. The woman's good intentions might cause circumstances to turn the wrong way. "Please, Mrs. Olsen. We've decided to let the police handle this."

"I'm just giving them a helping hand." She patted Darcie's arm. "Don't worry about a thing."

Darcie fought back a giggle as the woman rushed up the stairs. Don't worry? What about being used as bait? Or falling in love with your boss? Or, the million-dollar question; what about a relationship with a God who might ask her to give up everything she held dear?

She snorted in her attempt not to laugh. When York took a step toward her, she raised a hand. "I'm…all right. Really. Besides losing my mind."

"It's too much. I'll call Roger and tell him the deal is off." York took her hands in his.

"No." Darcie took a deep breath. "It feels good to laugh." She snorted again at the concerned look on his face. "I'm sorry. My emotions are whirling." As quick as the laughter overtook, so did the tears. "I've been dead for so long, now I feel like I'm starting to live, and I don't know how. It's like every emotion is trying to come out all at the same time." She covered her face with her hands. "I'm not making any sense. I'm going to bed." She attempted a smile and trudged up the stairs.

After closing her bedroom door, Darcie headed to the shower. Letting her clothes fall in a pile to the floor she turned the faucet on and stepped beneath the hot spray. The water mingled with her tears. When she realized she cried from happiness, she opened her eyes then quickly closed them, choosing to smile instead.

Happy. A concept not familiar to her, but one she looked forward to growing accustomed to. She turned off the water and moved to the bedroom where the simple cotton gown she slept in waited. She slipped it over head then climbed beneath the cool sheets.

She stared at the paneled ceiling and contemplated the words in York's leather Bible. It'd been like reading a love story. One written for her. Darcie wrapped her arms around her stomach. She'd read of a love so strong even death couldn't defeat it.

Tomorrow could be the end of her past life, and the beginning of something wonderful. She almost looked forward to it.

# CHAPTER TWENTY-SIX

Darcie woke to Sam and Sarah's chattering as they made their way downstairs. She smiled, refreshed, and rolled from bed to don a tank top and long jean shorts. She subdued her curls into a ponytail and made her way to the kitchen where York scrambled eggs at the stove.

He greeted her with a grin. Humor lines radiated from the corners of his eyes. "Gotta to eat fast if we're going to meet Roger. Today's the day, Darcie. The day we end all this."

Hope leaped in her chest. She prayed he was right. With the help of police officers, surely they'd find Tony's package, apprehend the ones responsible for the crimes, and begin a new life. Whether or not Darcie's new life contained the Wardell family was left to be seen. She hoped so. But, she was determined to try the waiting on God thing. She'd start with her future.

"Good morning." She accepted the plate York handed her and took a place at the table. When was the last time someone cooked her breakfast? She wracked her brain. Not since her grandmother. "I could get used to being waited on."

"I'd like you to get used to it." York winked. "You ready for today?"

"As ready as I can be." She dipped a fork into the fluffy eggs, warmed by his words as much as the food. Was she ready to put herself in front of a possible sniper's bullet? She knew what being used for bait could entail. *I'm trying to trust you, Lord. I really am.*

"Great." He set his plate at the head of the table. "Let's eat and get this day started."

Breakfast eaten and dishes washed, Darcie followed York and the kids outside. Her gaze kept flicking to the rifle crooked in York's arm. "Do you need that? The cops will be armed, won't they?"

"I'm not taking any chances." He moved the Ford's front seat forward so Sam and Sarah could climb in. "We'll all be searching for that elusive envelope, box, whatever. It's better to be prepared."

Darcie shoved down the rising apprehension, refusing to give up her resolve to not be afraid. She slid into her seat and clicked the seatbelt across her. "What are the kids going to do?"

"Stay close by us." He reached over and squeezed her hand. "We'll be fine. This is almost over. Relax."

She nodded. "Okay." Despite the resolve to be calm, butterflies stampeded through her stomach. By the time they'd reached Tony's family's hunting cabin, her insides were twisted in knots and perspiration dotted her upper lip.

Roger and two other men in civilian clothes milled around the weed grown patch of land the wood-shingled building sat on. That's all he brought? Darcie's high spirits threatened to drop.

Two others? Were they even police? She'd expected a small army. She shoved her door open and stepped into the morning sunshine.

Locusts buzzed from the stand of trees surrounding them. A light breeze whispered through the branches. Murmurs from the searchers rolled over her. Darcie studied the small building in front of her. Shack was a good name for it. She pulled the key Anthony had given her from her pocket and stared at the front door hanging from its hinges. She scoffed at Tony's father's idea of coming to check on the condition of the place. The best thing to do would be bulldoze it to the ground and start over. She shoved the key back in her pocket.

Sam and Sarah dashed past, heading for a fallen-down structure that might have once been a shed of some kind. York called after them to stay by his or Darcie's side.

"I'll keep them with me." Darcie laid an arm around each child's shoulders. "They can help me look. You go talk to Roger."

"You sure?"

She nodded and led the children toward the back of the cabin. A rock-lined well sat off to one side. The top rungs of a ladder stuck over the edge. Darcie peered into the dark recess. The ladder looked dry and cracked. The musty odor of old dirt wafted upwards. Sam dropped a rock in the hole. A dull thud echoed as it hit bottom.

"Let's go dig around in that old shed."

Sam and Sarah ran ahead of her. Sam grabbed a stick from the ground and trailed it behind him, leaving a thin track in the dirt. Sarah stooped and grabbed a handful of flowering weeds then ran back and thrust them in Darcie's hands.

"Aren't they pretty?" Her gap-toothed smile brought tears to Darcie's eyes.

"Yes, they are. Thank you." Darcie held them at arm's length, her nose already itching. She laid a hand over her heart, marveling at how quickly Sam and Sarah filled part of it and helped push away the empty places.

She turned at York's voice raised in anger.

~

"I won't do it, Roger." York's face heated. "Not in front of the cabin. Alone. You might as well paint a bulls-eye on her!"

"I just want her visible. She isn't while she's back there." Roger waved his arm in Darcie's direction. "What did you think my plan entailed?"

"She's caring for my children. That's her job." York shook his head and paced. Dust flew around his feet. Officer or not, Roger was certifiably insane. It had taken everything in York's will power to keep an upbeat mood to the morning. Driving out here tossed all his work in the garbage and nailed down the lid.

"You're more interested in catching this crook than you are in protecting a life." York whirled to face Roger. "Has your career gotten so important you've forgotten the value of a person?"

"Putting this guy away will prevent a lot of others from suffering Suzy's fate. Or Darcie's husband's." Roger squared his shoulders. "I'm going to do what gets the job done. I'm armed. So are my men." His head motioned toward York's rifle propped against the cabin. "And you have a weapon. We're as prepared as we're going to be. But I want Leroy's men to know Darcie is here."

"They'll know without us parading her out front. This is a small town. People talk and thanks to my housekeeper, everyone in town knows there are men looking for Darcie." York grabbed fistfuls of his hair. What could he say to convince the other man of Darcie's danger? He didn't want to look on her lifeless body. Gunned down by a killer. His world had turned to madness. Shifting from one dramatic plot line to another. Lord, help him.

Darcie stepped into sight. "Fine. I'll stand out here, doing absolutely nothing, while the rest of you search. York can stand guard." She speared Roger with a golden glance. "You do know how ridiculous that sounds, right? Two less people to look for what Tony hid."

Roger shrugged. "It's more important to put Leroy behind bars."

"And you don't think Tony's list might accomplish that?" She dropped to the top sagging step.

"Wait a minute." York felt like a light bulb exploded over his head. "There's more here than you're telling us, Roger. You have a personal stake in this. What lit your tail on fire? Do you have your own gambling problems to bear?"

"No. Leroy ruined my father." Roger spun on one heel and marched away.

York remembered the story. Or at least the version released to the public. Five years ago, Roger's family lost the proverbial family farm. Everyone assumed it was because Roger's father lost his job.

A few months later, he'd been found dead, in his car, in Shadow Lake. Roger's mother never recovered from the shock. She followed soon after, dead from an overdose of sleeping pills. His friend had endured a tragic life. One York felt compassion for, but that didn't give the man reason to endanger the woman York loved.

Darcie sat slumped shouldered. York lowered himself beside her and put an arm around her. "You don't need to do this. Not because Roger has a personal vendetta."

"I know." She lifted her gaze skyward and closed her eyes. The breeze teased the curls around her face. "I can't live until this is over, York. I want to learn about a life with God. Not one where I just hear about Him. Does that make sense?"

He hugged her. "Perfectly." His children's laughter carried to him, reassuring him of their safety behind the protection of the building. "Let me get my rifle and be your shining knight."

She giggled. "You do that. I'll be the frail damsel in distress. We'll write our own ending to this story. A happy one."

He placed a kiss on her forehead. Her skin warm and smooth beneath his lips.

He rose and reached for his rifle as a dark sedan sped up the road. York's heart stopped as he caught a glimpse of a gun's barrel. He lunged in front of Darcie.

A shot rang out.

A searing fire burned through him, and his world went black.

# CHAPTER TWENTY-SEVEN

Events seemed to click in slow motion. York stepped in front of Darcie. A shot rang out.

He spun. His head collided with the step. The thump of old wood meeting skull vibrated through his head. Gunfire erupted from both sides of the house.

Sarah's scream split the air.

Darcie fought the urge to kneel beside York or run for the kids. Against everything in her, every emotion pulling her toward the man lying bleeding at her feet, she whirled, leaped off the porch, then sprinted to the back yard. "Sam! Sarah!" She frantically searched the area. The children huddled beneath a bush. Darcie grabbed their hands and yanked them to her side.

Where could they go? The front lawn sounded like a war. Popping as frantic as microwave popcorn. Yells. Curses. An officer dashed in their direction, and fell. His hand stretched toward Darcie and the kids.

Spotting the ladder sticking up over the well, Darcie shoved the children ahead of her. "Into the well. Now."

"Where's Daddy?" Sarah clutched Darcie's shirt.

"In front. With the other men." *God, please let him be alive.*

Sam and Sarah scurried down as nimble as monkeys. Darcie gripped the top rung, slung a leg over, and stared, white-knuckled, below her. From the inky recesses of the hole, the children's pale faces looked up at her. She could do this. For them, she could go into the small dark space. She shook her head and plastered herself against the rough wood of the ladder. No, she couldn't.

A bullet gouged the mortar by her hand. Darcie yelped. Her foot slipped. Her body slammed against the rock walls, knocking the breath from her. She flailed her legs until she gained a foothold. Hand over hand, foot beneath foot, she made her way until damp dirt met her shaky legs.

Sam and Sarah launched themselves at her, knocking her to her knees. The odor of dank, old air filled her nostrils. The rapid shooting and cries from above became muffled and farther apart. Darcie stared at the light-filled circle above them, hoping, praying for a sight of York's face. No other gunman appeared so she assumed the bullet had been a random shot.

She drew a shuddery breath. God wouldn't do it twice, would He? Take away the man she cared for? Darcie scooted backwards until she leaned against the well side. She pulled Sam and Sarah with her, tucking them beneath her arms.

No child would die this time. Not like Davey. These two children would live to be hugged another day.

A sob caught in her throat. They needed their father. Not their nanny. Not a woman who ran from life like a fox dashed away from a hound. *York, where are you? Show yourself. Let me know you're okay.*

"I want my daddy." Sarah cried, the sobs turning into hiccups.

Darcie tightened her hold on the girl. "We'll stay down here until it's safe. Then we'll go to him." Her chest hurt with the struggle not to cry herself. "Right now, we need to stay here and be quiet. Can you do that?"

Sarah nodded. Sam rose and stood at the foot of the ladder. "I'll keep watch. Let you know if anyone comes. Listen. The shooting is stopping."

Darcie smiled at his attempt to be the protector. Ten years old and so much like his father it stabbed Darcie's heart. When they could leave their damp prison, how would she tell them about their father being shot?

Silence reigned above them. What did it mean? Safety or danger? Who'd won the battle?

Her gaze roamed the walls. The setting sun highlighted a niche.

Darcie propped a sleepily nodding Sarah upright. She stood on tiptoes and pulled a manila envelope from the crack. Lifting the flap, Darcie pulled a sheet of paper and micro-sized cassette from the pouch. She'd found it!

Too dark to see the writing, she slid everything back where she'd found it. When someone came for them, she'd finally have what they'd been looking for.

Roger could arrest the ones involved and life would move on. Darcie's knees sagged. What if Roger were dead? His men? York? She put a fist to her mouth to stifle a cry. When would they know it was safe to emerge from the well?

She'd have to wait and trust God. Everywhere she turned, that concept popped up. Now she waited frightened with two terrified children at the bottom of a dry well.

Keeping an eye on the form of Sam still playing sentry, she sat back down next to Sarah and laid the little girl's head in her lap. The motion of smoothing Sarah's hair calmed her. Gave her something to do besides wait and stare at the round circle of fading light. Sam was right. The gunfire had stopped.

Why didn't anyone come for them? How long should they stay down here?

Locusts sang above their prison. Occasionally, the neon glow of a lightening bug drifted across the well's mouth. A bull frog croaked. Normal noises. Comforting in their solidarity and commonness.

"Should I go up and look around?" Sam asked without turning.

"No!" The thought of him wandering around with Darcie not knowing who'd emerged victorious, the law or criminals, chilled her heart. "We wait."

"I don't like waiting."

"Neither do I." Darcie let her head fall back. She closed her eyes. *Okay, God. I'm going to try this prayer thing. For some reason, you've put me here in this time and place. In this danger. Maybe like York said, I'm here to put these men away. If that is my purpose, please don't let anyone I care about die. Please bring York back to me, and give me the strength to go through whatever you want me to.*

A siren wailed, growing in intensity. A car engine cranked to life. Darcie strained to hear. Gravel crunched. The killers were leaving? Were the others alive or dead? "Sam, get over here by Sarah. I'm going up."

Darcie paused halfway up the ladder. "If I'm not back soon, wait until morning before you leave the well. At daylight, find your way to Mrs. Olsen's."

"But you're coming back, right?" Sam's voice shook.

"God willing, Sam." Darcie proceeded up the ladder and peered over the well's lip. Moonlight cast shadows over the lawn. Silence echoed. She grunted as she pulled herself over and crouched.

Not hearing anything, she rose and snuck around the house. An ambulance backed out of the drive and sped down the highway, sirens blaring.

One man stood staring in the direction of the road, hand tucked beneath his arm. Another slumped against the porch railing.

"Roger?"

The man standing whirled. "Darcie! Where have you been?"

She'd never been so glad to see a police officer in her life. "In the well. Sam and Sarah are still there. Where's York?"

"Gone. Along with my other man." Roger coughed. "The perpetrators got away, but we managed to wound one of them."

Gone. The single word froze her heart as cold as marble. Her knees buckled. Roger caught her in his good arm. "Hold on, Darcie. Another ambulance is on its way."

"I don't need one. The envelope is in the well. A manila envelope stuffed into a hole." Darcie grabbed his shirt in both hands. "Was it worth it? The shooting, the bloodshed?" Her voice rose to a shriek. "The fall of York and your man?" She released him and sat on the steps, her face buried in her hands. *God, where are you?*

"Are you sure it's the information we're seeking?"

How could the man be so insensitive? "I didn't read it, if that's what you're asking. It's dark down there." She rose and wiped her face on her dirty sleeve. York's cell phone lay in the dirt at her feet. Darcie picked it up and slipped it into her pocket. "I'm going to get Sam and Sarah. There's no need for them to be down there any longer." *God, what do I tell them about York?*

She couldn't believe Roger's selfishness. For the second time in her life, the man she'd given her heart to was gone. All the officer in charge cared about was Tony's infamous package. If she had a gun, she'd be tempted to shoot the man and hang the consequences. But for now, the children needed her.

With heavy steps she made her way back to

where Sam and Sarah waited. Exhaustion wore on her. Her head pounded. She rested a minute before bending over the waist-high wall. Before she could call down, a car roared up the driveway. She ducked as it stopped in front of the house and two men got out with guns drawn. They yelled for Roger and the other officer to drop their weapons. Darcie scuttled across the yard until she crouched close enough to hear them order Roger and the other man to kneel with their hands behind their heads.

They were going to kill them. Darcie leaped to her feet and sprinted around the house, hands held in front of her. "Wait! I know where the list and tape are. Please, no more killing. Let these men go, and I'll go with you."

The men turned, pistols pointed in her direction.

# CHAPTER TWENTY-EIGHT

"Well, well." The uninjured of the two men, the one who'd spoken with her at Suzy's barbecue, leered. "Guess we did have the wrong girl, Jack." He gripped her arm. "Just tell us where it is, and we'll kill you quick. You pigs drop your weapons and kick them to me, or I shoot this pretty little thing right here in front of you."

Roger and his officer complied, keeping their hands in sight. Roger's face paled. Blood dripped from his hand. His gaze flicked from Darcie to the armed men.

Darcie tried pulling free but her arm remained firmly encased in the man's fist. "I'll take you there. But only if you leave these men alone."

"Darcie, you don't have to do this." Roger made a move toward her and stopped when the man sporting a wound in his shoulder, waved him back.

"I'd like nothing more than to put another bullet

in you, cop man. Can I, Pete?"

"Take care of Sam and Sarah, Roger." Darcie glanced at him. "And call York." She mouthed, "I have his phone."

He nodded in understanding, the frown not leaving his face. "I hope you know what you're doing."

"Enough talk. I'm bleeding here and need to get some medical attention." Jack shot out the tires on Roger's squad car. "We'll be long gone before you get those fixed." Darcie shrank back at his crazed laugh.

Sirens wailed in the distance.

"Let's go." Darcie found herself yanked along and shoved in the backseat of the criminal's car. "Not a peep out of you."

"Do I get to at least have a proper introduction? I'd like to know who I'm riding with." She caught herself before she slammed into the opposite door.

"I'm Pete, and the hurt one is Jack." The big bald man turned the key in the ignition and jammed the gear shift into drive. "No more talking. Leroy don't like talkative women. Now tell us where it's hidden."

"I'll tell Leroy. He's the boss, right?" Obviously her statement stumped the buffoons in the front seat. They stared at each other a moment. Darcie crossed her arms, hoping to hide their trembling. Acting tough might be her best defense. Helpless would get her killed sooner. She had to make them believe they needed her.

"Who put the warning note in my barn?"

"That would be me." Pete, the driver, said. "We

was watching you and that other broad. Wasn't sure which of you was the right one. Jack didn't leave no note. Said it was too dangerous."

"Shut up, Pete. That ain't none of her business." Jack leaned his head against the window.

Ten minutes later, sweat pouring down her face, Darcie straightened in her seat. "Where are we going? Could you turn on the air-conditioner?"

"None of your business, and it don't work."

The man, Jack, slumped in the passenger-side front seat. Each bump in the road elicited a groan from him. His wiry body seemed smaller than before as he hunched over.

"Your friend needs a doctor." Darcie leaned her arms along the seat in front of her. "Maybe we should stop at the hospital."

Pete tossed a heated glance over his shoulder. "Maybe you should shut up and tell us where that package is."

Darcie forced a smile to her lips. "Well, which is it? Shut up or tell you where it is?"

"You're a smart mouth, you are." He clapped Jack on the shoulder. "Leroy is going to love her."

Considering the lack of brain matter in the heads of her present captors, Darcie didn't want to meet the infamous Leroy, master-mind behind it all. She didn't think playing tough would work with him. Being frightened wouldn't be a struggle. If not for the tight clenching of her jaw, she'd give into tears.

What would she tell Leroy about the envelope? Would he kill her when she informed him it was back at the cabin? Should she make up some other destination to buy time? By then, Roger would have had enough time to get the children to safety.

She hadn't checked the bars on York's phone and prayed it had enough charge that she could turn it on once they stopped. *Please, God, let Roger have understood what I meant when I said to call York.* With the phone on, they could trace her. She'd read that somewhere. How much time did the police need? Could she stall long enough?

Tears stung her eyes, and she cupped a hand over the bulge in her pocket. The phone was her only solid connection to York. Should she have tried to save him?

Maybe Sam and Sarah would have been okay behind the house. She shook her head. No, York would've wanted her to look after them first.

"Why are your eyes red? Aw, man. You ain't crying are you?" Pete's gaze met hers through the rearview mirror. "I hate crying women. Waste of time. A down-right nuisance."

"Sorry to inconvenience you." Darcie wiped her eyes on her dirty sleeve. She must look a fright. Wild hair, red-eyes, and dirty face. Maybe she could scare Leroy into leaving her alone.

Who was she kidding? She lived on borrowed time. She had ever since the car accident.

She thought back to the night she'd met York. Standing there on the edge of the mountain, she'd seriously considered jumping. Cowardice prevented her. If she'd been brave enough, York would still be with his children. Her shoulders shook with the sobs she tried holding in.

Now that love once again entered into her life, death wasn't something she craved. God gave her a gift, the desire for life with a wonderful family. She brushed a hand over her stomach. The loss didn't feel as strong, as consuming. God had begun the healing process. Darcie sniffed. Now, in what felt like her eleventh hour, she felt His love. Remembered His promises. She still didn't see how anything good could come of her circumstances, but she'd try to trust Him. Again.

At the realization that for the first time in over a year, Darcie wanted to live, really live, caused laughter to burst from her. It bubbled up from her core and spilled out with the force of an erupting volcano.

"What the…" Pete jerked the wheel. "You want to cause an accident? Stop that noise! Hey, Jack, we've got us a crazy woman. Jack? You asleep?" Pete took one hand off the wheel and shook his partner. Jack tumbled into him.

"He's dead." Pete whipped the steering wheel to the right, stopping the car on the shoulder of the highway.

"I told you we should get him to a hospital." Darcie forced her laughter to subside to giggles, then a choked sob. What was she doing here? With a corpse just inches from her? She clutched her stomach and rocked.

"Shut up!" Pete jammed the gear shift into park then wrapped his shining head in his large hands. "I can't think with that racket."

His ability to think at any time was hard for Darcie to believe. At any moment, she expected steam to blow from his over-sized ears. He turned to glare at her, effectively halting her laugh.

"Shove him out of the car."

"What?"

Pete reached for the gun he'd laid on the dashboard and swung it to point at her. "Climb over the seat and push him out."

"I will not. You do it. It's your fault he's dead."

"I can't. He's my partner. It wouldn't be right. If you don't do it, I'll shoot you here and both of you can lie in the ditch. Now get to it!"

Why couldn't the bigger, more obnoxious guy have been the one shot? Darcie climbed over the seat, gaining satisfaction when her knee collided with Pete's jaw. A curse exploded from his mouth, and he jabbed her in the ribs with his gun.

Nausea rose as she leaned over Jack to open the door. The sour stench of perspiration and the metallic odor of blood threatened to choke her. From the back seat, the smell had been bearable. Leaning over the body, was atrocious. Darcie lived a nightmare.

When the door swung open, she planted both of her palms against Jack's shoulder and shoved. He hit the pavement with a thud and rolled into a weed-grown ditch. Her upset stomach won. Darcie lurched toward the door and lost the little food left in her stomach.

Pete grabbed the waistband of her shorts and yanked her inside. "Get in the back. I don't want you up here distracting me." He leered. "Thirty more minutes, and you'll be Leroy's problem."

Darcie fell into the back, climbed onto the seat, and wrapped her arms around her knees. She didn't think the feel of Jack's dead body would ever leave her. Her hands were sticky with his blood. She rubbed them vigorously down her shorts. She wanted out of the car and away from Pete. She didn't want to meet Leroy. She wanted York.

Exhaustion from the pretense of being tough overwhelmed her. The last ounce of her strength waned as she fought to remain upright and not give into despair. Forget leading the authorities to Leroy. She'd bolt the next time the car stopped.

This part of the Ozark had plenty of trees, even scattered amongst the buildings of small cities. She'd find a place to hide. Her efforts would narrow the police's search. They could find Leroy on their own. Darcie turned her head and rested her cheek on her bent knees. Her eyes closed.

Pete knocked on her head, startling her awake. He grinned. "We're here."

# CHAPTER TWENTY-NINE

They'd stopped in front of what appeared to be a strip of abandoned shops and offices. Despite the grip of frost encasing Darcie's heart, she couldn't help but compare the location to every detective or gangster movie she'd ever seen. The absence of other cars chilled her to the pit of her stomach. She slipped her hand into her pocket and pressed the on button to York's phone. *Please, God, let the phone have a full charge and be on vibrate.*

Pete grabbed his gun from the dashboard. "Get out. No funny stuff. I ain't afraid to shoot."

As if she could forget. She shoved open her door and planted her feet on asphalt hot enough to feel through her sneakers.

Pete waved her ahead of him into a concrete room containing a single metal chair and some crates. She eyed the floor.

More painted cement. No dust, no grease marks.

No insects skittered across their path. Most likely it made things easier to clean up after they tortured her. A single light bulb swung from the raftered ceiling.

"Sit. And you'd better be sitting when Leroy comes. He don't take kindly to things not going his way." Pete's laugh resonated in the empty room.

Darcie sat, then bolted to her feet as soon as the door locked behind his retreating form. She scanned the room. She'd need to hide the phone. Empty-headed Pete hadn't thought to search her. She had no such qualms about his boss.

A sliver of a window sat two feet above her head. She dragged the chair beneath it. She climbed up and slid the phone as far back on the ledge as her fingers would reach. She'd just replaced the chair when footsteps approached. She plopped back down, and stared at the floor.

Her heart threatened to beat from her chest. She counted slowly, trying to control her breathing. If she didn't, she feared she'd hyperventilate. Cooperation seemed the key from what she'd heard about Richard Leroy. *God, help me.*

Pete entered first, followed by a man over six feet tall, wearing a dark suit, and auburn hair slicked back from a chiseled face. Too harsh to be handsome, but striking nevertheless. No softness marred his look as he glared at Darcie.

"She's filthy." The man sneered. "I can't stand to look at her. Did you search this woman?"

Pete shook his head, eyes wide. "She's feisty, sir. I don't think she'd let me."

"You have a gun, idiot. Don't ask permission.

Search her.”

Darcie swallowed against the Mt. Everest size lump in her throat and stood, arms at her side. Thank God, she'd gotten rid of the phone. She closed her eyes and endured the clumsy patting and poking from Pete.

“She's clean.”

“Far from it.” Leroy marched and stood so close to her, Darcie had no option but to fall back in the chair. “Where's the list?”

“What…list?” Darcie cringed.

“Pete.” Leroy inclined his head. “Get the information out of her.”

“I ain't hitting no woman, boss.” Pete's face reddened.

Darcie jerked upright. Pete had morals after all. If she'd known, maybe she could've taken advantage in the car, before they arrived here. She wanted to slap herself. Stupid.

“You'll do as you're told.” Leroy whipped his head and speared Pete with a steely glance.

“Come on. Make it easy on yourself. Where's the list?” The look on Pete's face was almost pleading.

Darcie shrugged.

“You said you knew where it was!” Pete tapped her cheek. More like a pat from an affectionate uncle than a brutal gunman.

Darcie licked her lips and grinned. “I lied.”

Pete used his backhand a bit harder, and Darcie let her head fall back, pretending the slap actually hurt. Her grin widened. “I just wanted to keep you from killing anyone else.”

Leroy cursed and paced. “You, Pete, have got to

be the dumbest thug I've ever hired. She's played you for the fool. She's lying. She knows where it is."

Darcie raised her eyebrows. "Prove it." Her heart sped up its the rock 'n roll tempo until she thought they'd see it beating through her tee shirt.

"No need." Leroy smiled with as much warmth as a shark. "Pete is going to tie you to the chair and leave you to rot until you tell me what I want to know." He rolled his head around his neck. "This room gets very cold at night. I'll be sitting snug in my hotel room, enjoying a fine glass of wine with a pretty woman, while you sit and contemplate your circumstances."

"I need to use the restroom first."

Leroy glared. "Pete, get Shelly. We need a woman with her. I wouldn't want to offend your sensibilities."

"Thank you, boss." Pete scurried from the room.

Leroy stopped his pacing. "While you're in there, clean yourself up. Tomorrow, regardless of how dirty you might be, I'll resume interrogating you myself. I won't feel the same way as Pete about knocking you off that chair. Understood?"

Darcie nodded. She'd have to find a way out before then. She lowered her head. Not only did she feel as if she were in a nightmare, but in the surreal surroundings of a cheap dime-store mystery novel. Thugs, chair, concrete room, complete with a woman named Shelly. Darcie bit her tongue. The pain assured her it wasn't a dream. "Whatever you say, boss."

"Don't ridicule me, girl." Leroy spun on his

finely shined shoes and marched from the room, his steps echoing.

Darcie sagged and let the tears she'd been holding inside fall. What about cooperation? One look at Leroy and she'd resumed the tough girl image. The one she'd used her entire life when things were out of her control. All she had to do was open her mouth and tell them where the envelope was. No big deal. What did it matter to her? The children were safe, York was gone, and her stubbornness could get her killed.

The room grew darker and Darcie's bladder fuller. Had they forgotten her? She rose from the chair, and with outstretched hands, felt her way along the walls in the direction of the door. She tried the knob. Locked, as she'd expected. She banged on the door. "Hey! Anyone there?"

They wouldn't really leave her alone all night, would they? In the dark?

A whimper rose in her throat. Something scurried to her right. Were there mice? Waiting for her to fall asleep so they could bite? Darcie gnawed her lower lip and plastered her back to the cool wall. She couldn't remember seeing a light switch. Facing the dark cavernous room, she scooted along the wall, feeling for a switch.

The light from the small window disappeared like a curtain lowering inch by inch, leaving her in darkness so complete she couldn't distinguish her hand in front of her face from the wall. Her whimpers grew louder. Horrible visions of childhood, hiding from her mother and visitors, ripped through her mind. Darcie slid to the floor and huddled against the falling temperatures.

Her skin crawled, remembering how her mother's visitors had looked at her as she grew. Her body developing despite the baggy clothes she'd taken to wearing. Her mother always kept the men away from her. The one major point she'd scored as a mother. Escape to the roomed in back porch or tree house had been Darcie's retreat to an imaginary world of her own making. One where her mother loved her and her brother grew healthy and strong.

Grandma said God watched over her, even in the midst of childhood terror. Darcie hadn't believed her then. Now, with Pete's reluctance to touch her, Darcie felt more assured of God's protecting hand. She squirmed in an effort to get comfortable.

Leroy would leave her here to wet her pants, freeze to death, and lose her mind in the darkness. Not to mention a stomach rumbling with hunger and fear. Another skittering noise reminded Darcie she wasn't completely alone, and she drew her knees as close to her chest as physically possible. The chill from the concrete floor seeped into her bones, and she shivered.

Closing her eyes, she resorted to her childhood way of passing time. Counting from a hundred, backwards. Then the same with the alphabet. When she finished, she started over. It didn't seem to comfort the same way. At least then, she could hear the forest animals, or the rumble of her mother's voice as she entertained. Here, nothing but silence, and the occasional scurry met her ears.

She should've read more of York's Bible. Then she could've recited verses of comfort. Words of safety. Her grandmother's voice rang as clear as if the dear woman stood in the same room. "Sometimes, God lets us hit bottom, so we can see the top. So we can see Him."

Well, Darcie couldn't think of a bottom any lower than the one she'd hit. She'd thought losing Tony and her unborn child had been bad. It was nothing compared to this. Shut up alone in inky blackness. The man she loved dead. The children who quickly claimed a large part of her heart were being consoled by someone else. Tears burned down Darcie's frigid cheeks.

*Lord, if you can hear me in this place, if my words can reach through these block walls, send me a sign. Some way that I can know You're there. That You haven't forgotten me.*

The door clicked open beside her. The light glared overhead, blinding her. Darcie blinked against the glare. "Mother?"

# CHAPTER THIRTY

Blond, dressed in linen pants and a low-cut silk turquoise blouse, Maggie McGee lounged in the doorway, a cigarette dangling from her fingers, and looking worlds away from what she'd been during Darcie's childhood. This woman was pampered down to her ruby-red toenails. "Richard said you needed to use the restroom."

Darcie stared. That's it?

In fifteen years Maggie hadn't bothered to contact her only daughter, and that's all she had to say? Darcie brushed past her, catching a whiff of a soft, exotic fragrance almost overpowered by the stink of cigarette smoke. "You seem to have done well for yourself."

Maggie shrugged. "Richard takes good care of me. The restroom is to the right. It isn't much but there's running water. These buildings haven't been used in a while. Take this opportunity to clean up.

There's another shirt for your use. Richard is already going to be upset if Pete doesn't get the car cleaned out before picking him up tomorrow. He hates filth."

"Gee, thanks, Mom." Darcie shoved open the door, leaving her mother standing outside. Unfortunately, the door had no lock, and Maggie followed her.

"I'm supposed to keep an eye on you." Maggie leaned against one of the wall-hanging sinks. "So, how have you been?"

Darcie paused as she bent over the basin. "You want to make small talk? Fine." She straightened and crossed her arms. "I got married to Tony Thayer, but I'm sure you know all about that. We had an accident. He died, along with my unborn baby. How are you? And now am I to assume my dead husband was mixed up with you? This is too much to think about. How does it feel being mixed up with a man like Richard Leroy?"

"I've had worse." Maggie took a drag from her cigarette, tossed the butt in the sink, and reached into her cleavage for the pack. "Sorry about your kid. Losing a child is…difficult. And rest at ease, I never had contact with Tony."

"Right." Darcie turned on the faucet, forced herself not to dwell on the pain radiating from her bladder, and splashed tepid water on her face. The stench from the nearby stall almost curbed her need for release.

A navy tee-shirt, several sizes too big, hung on a nail beside the sink. Darcie yanked off the sweat-stained one she wore and tossed it into the nearest trash can before donning the clean shirt. "I'm ready. Where's Leroy?"

"You won't be seeing him until tomorrow."

"Great." Darcie shoved open a stained stall. Revulsion choked her at the sight of the rusty, cracked toilet. "Something to look forward to."

Bladder relieved, she rejoined her mother. "What now?"

Maggie shrugged again. "He won't kill you when he finds out you're my daughter, but I'd really advise you to change your attitude."

"Can't you even look at me when you talk?" Darcie didn't know what she felt for the woman standing in front of her. Pity, maybe. Certainly not the love a daughter should feel for her mother. Why should she care how Maggie McGee treated her? They'd already had the longest conversation Darcie could remember.

Maggie's gaze flicked to her. "You look like your father."

"I'm surprised you know who my father is."

"Of course, I know. He was the lead bass player for some fifty-cent band wannabes. A woman and baby didn't fit in with his plans. He split. End of story. Are you finished in here? This room is disgusting. Pete's waiting to take you to my motel room."

"Why couldn't I clean up there?"

Maggie shrugged. "Richard has this fetish about cleanliness. He said for you to change, so you changed."

"Why doesn't Leroy know I'm your daughter?"

"I'll tell him in the morning. Just keep in mind

that Pete will be standing guard outside the room so you won't be able to run." Maggie's steps faltered. "And don't call me mother until I've had a chance to warn Richard. He doesn't like surprises."

"Perfect." The thought of sleeping in a bed rather than the dark concrete cave filled Darcie with hope. Maybe she could even get a meal out of her mother.

Maggie led her to the same car Pete had driven earlier. Darcie eyed the front seat before climbing in the back. Cleaned of any evidence of Jack's injuries. She clicked her seatbelt across her, and remembered York's phone. How would Roger find her now?

Pete sped from the vacant parking lot, the street lights the only sign of life in a small town gone to sleep. The closest motel Darcie could think of was five miles away. Would Roger think to look there?

"This one's gone quiet all of a sudden." Pete motioned his head in Darcie's direction. "On the way here, all she did was yak. I wanted to smack her around, make her shut up, ya know?"

"Sure you did." Maggie lit a cigarette and blew the smoke out her open window. "Now that she's not talking, you will?"

"Well, no, I…" Pete glowered and hunched over the steering wheel.

Darcie smiled and settled back in her seat. Wouldn't that be a twist of circumstances? Her mother coming to her defense after all these years? God had a strange sense of humor. As long as He stayed on Darcie's side, she'd try to roll with the punches and trust Him.

She wanted York's reassurance things would be

fine. That God never left his children. This strange new "mother" figure sitting in front of her filled Darcie with misgivings. What kind of game was the woman playing?

"Shelly. That's your name, right?" Sounded like a gangster's moll. The thought left a bitter taste in Darcie's mouth.

"That's right." Maggie released another plume of smoke.

"Why is Leroy letting you take me to the motel instead of the warehouse? Is he trying to get my cooperation by bribing me with luxury?" Darcie fingered the worn tee shirt she wore. "Like this fine piece of fabric here?"

Maggie turned and glared. "No more talking." She cut her eyes at Pete.

Darcie had no choice but to sit back and see how things played out. Maybe she could gain her mother's sympathy. Tony's envelope, hopefully now in Roger's possession, became more important to her survival. Putting Leroy away would also mean Maggie's arrest. If she could convince her mother to flee with her, Darcie would call Roger and let him know Leroy's whereabouts.

Pete pulled into the motel Darcie hoped he would. "Act like we're one big happy family, and I won't have to shove the gun in your back."

"No problem." Darcie strolled behind her mother, Pete behind her.

Maggie unlocked the room door and waved them inside. Two queen beds with gold quilted bedspreads, brown shag carpet, and a framed print depicting an autumn scene. Darcie had stayed in better places on her way to Shadow Springs.

"Leroy must be a big spender." She plopped on the edge of the nearest bed.

"He got the closest he could to that rinky-dink town." Maggie lowered herself to a chair beside a round laminate table and lit another cigarette. "I'm sure we'll be out of here by morning."

Great. The room already smelled like stale cigarettes. Now, she'd have to breathe the gray haze too. Darcie's gaze flicked to the phone then to Pete standing sentry at the window. "Hey, Pete. Could you run out and get me something to eat? It wouldn't look good if Leroy's prize prisoner died of starvation."

"Nope. Not supposed to leave."

"Good grief." Maggie flicked her ashes in a paper cup. "Tie her leg to the bedpost and go get a pizza."

Darcie suppressed a grin. That would leave her hands free. Maggie glanced at her, then concentrated on another drag from her Marlboro.

"Well, if you think it'll be okay?"

Maggie batted her lashes and grinned. "I'm here, aren't I?"

He nodded. "Yeah. I'm hungry too." Pete ripped the sheers from behind the light-blocking curtains and fastened Darcie's ankle to the bedpost. "Stay put."

After he'd left, Maggie rose. "I'm taking a shower. Be a good girl, Darcie. Use your head."

Her mother may have been a drunk and a loose woman, but she'd never been stupid. Tears stung Darcie's eyes as she realized this was her mother's way of helping her. A gift. One Darcie had every intention of accepting.

She bent and struggled with the tight knot around her leg until she freed herself. The sound of running water reassured her she still had time. Maggie might be providing an opportunity, but she'd do her job if she walked out and Darcie was on the phone.

With shaking fingers, Darcie punched in the number to the police station. She almost sobbed when Roger answered.

"Roger."

"Darcie? Where are you? Do you still have York's phone? We've put a trace on it. I've got officers on the way."

"I don't have it anymore. I left it at the warehouse off Interstate 40. I'm at that motel outside of town. Pick me up on the highway." She heard the water shut off. "I've got to go. Please. Give me ten minutes."

"Hurry, Darcie. Once you're picked up, we'll close in."

"Leroy isn't here. I don't know where he is. See you in a few."

She spun as Maggie exited the bathroom, wrapped in a towel. The years had been kind to Darcie's mother, despite the hard lifestyle. Even without her layers of makeup, her skin lay smooth on rounded cheeks. Fine lines radiated from her eyes, and just the beginning of wrinkles around the lips.

Maggie frowned. "Now you're going to have to hit me or something. Why couldn't you have just left quickly?"

"I had to call for help. Come with me."

Her mother shook her head. "No, I'm ready for another adventure." A sad smile pulled at the corners of her mouth. "Jail is something I've managed to avoid until now. There always comes a time when your crimes catch up to you. I've sinned too many times to walk away." She motioned her head toward the phone. "Now hit me."

The tears rolled down Darcie's face. "I can't. Come with me. Turn yourself into the police. They'll be easier on you than Leroy will."

Maggie shook her head. "No." She tightened the towel more securely around her and lit a cigarette.

"I haven't done right by you, Darcie." She took a drag and released the smoke. "It's too late for Davey, and I'll suffer for that the rest of my life. But I can do one small thing for you. Take the opportunity." She rose and disappeared into the restroom.

Darcie whirled, fumbled with the lock on the door and dashed from the room. She ducked behind the dumpster as Pete pulled into the parking lot. As soon as he entered the room, she ran.

# CHAPTER THIRTY-ONE

"**G**et me out of here, Roger." York yanked the IV needle from his arm and winced at the sharp pain. He grabbed a tissue from a nearby box and pressed it in the crease of his elbow. "I know that call was Darcie. Either you take me with you, or I'll go on my own." He swung his legs over the side of the hospital bed, wincing at the ache in his shoulder. "And I owe you a punch in the face as soon as you take off that uniform."

"Get back in that bed." Roger stretched out his arm and pointed. "You don't know where she is."

"I'm going with you to find Darcie then I'm punching your lights out." York planted his feet on the floor and reached for his jeans.

"Man, you've been shot!"

"And I'm going to live. She needs me." Jeans on, York slipped out of the hospital gown and stared at his tee shirt folded on the nearby table. How would he wear it?

"We're wasting time." Roger laughed. "You'll never get that on over your head. Not with one arm bandaged."

"Then I'll go without." York stormed from the room, waved away the excited nurses, and marched out of the hospital. By the time he reached the sidewalk, spots swam before his eyes, and he leaned against Roger's squad car.

"I don't have time to pick you up off the street." Roger unclipped his radio and called for backup to meet him outside the Shadow Motel.

"Just open the door."

"Go away, York, before I have you arrested."

"Open the door!" York's head pounded the same as his fist on the car's roof.

"You are one pig-headed fool." Roger yanked the front passenger door open and let York slide in. "Don't bleed on the upholstery."

"Like you're one to talk." York leaned his head back against the seat and closed his eyes.

Fear for Darcie outweighed the burning agony in his shoulder. With Sam and Sarah safely with the Olsen's, his worry over Darcie had full rein on his emotions. *Please, God, protect her. Let us get there in time.*

He rolled his head to the side and glared at Roger's profile. "Did you get what you wanted?"

Roger nodded. "Thanks to Darcie. Stop looking at me like that. She saved my life. I intend to repay her by doing the same." He peeled from the parking lot, siren wailing. "When you have the use of both your arms, you can have a swing at me. But at least wait until I'm out of uniform."

York closed his eyes. "Oh, I will." The movement of the car made him nauseous. He'd have to remember the feeling to put in his novel. He'd have a lot of new scenarios to write about when this was over. Writing about things he knew took on an entirely different meaning.

Roger's cell phone rang, jarring him back to reality. "Yes, Doctor, I'm aware Mr. Wardell left the hospital without being released. He's in police custody as we speak. Yes, I'll bring him back as soon as I can." He shut his phone. "I need to get a new number. This town is too small for privacy."

York laughed and gasped against the pressure of his wound. "Yep, you have it really rough." He motioned at the bandage on Roger's hand. "How's your wound?"

"Just a graze."

"Uh-huh. Not following doctor's orders either, are you?"

"I will when this is over."

~

Darcie contemplated going back for her mother until she heard Pete's voice raised in anger. He sounded as if his aversion to hitting women might be at an end. Instead, she ran, her breath labored. *God, please spare Mom's life. As broken as she is, she's all I have.* Visions of York, Sam, and Sarah came to mind. Darcie smiled. Wrong. She had much more than she'd had a year ago.

By the time she'd dashed across the parking lot and reached the highway, her side ached, her heart pounded, and sweat ran in rivulets down her back.

A car engine roared to life, and she dove into the bushes.

Pete sped past, hunched over the steering wheel. Darcie raised up enough to glance in the direction of the motel. Maggie stood beside the door, looking in the direction Pete went. She ducked back into the room only to emerge seconds later with a suitcase in her hand. Chin held high, cigarette between the fingers of her free hand, she sauntered down the highway in the opposite direction from Darcie.

Darcie smiled. The McGee women had backbones after all. She was tempted to follow her mother, but the sound of a faraway, approaching police car drew her like the infamous singing sirens of the sea. She straightened and stepped onto the asphalt.

Roger squealed to a stop beside her and shut off his siren. Darcie's knees threatened to give way as York bolted from the passenger side. Tears streamed down her cheeks as he wrapped his unbandaged arm around her and pulled her against him.

"You're alive. But Roger said…" How could this be? She'd seen him shot and fall. He'd struck his head.

Roger yelled through the open door. "I said he was gone. Not dead. Y'all get in."

"Come on, sweetheart." York pulled her with him.

She shook her head. "Leroy is supposed to show up here sometime in the morning. We can still catch him. One of his goons is out right now, looking for me. If we wait, we'll catch them."

He continued dragging her with him until she found herself in the back seat. York followed, keeping his arm around her shoulders.

Roger slammed the car into gear and raced down the highway. "I'll have someone stationed here all night. We have to get York back to the hospital."

Darcie's heart plummeted. She gazed up at York. "I'll stay with you. The whole time, until you get out."

His arm tightened. "I'd like that. The doctor said I'd be out tomorrow. Don't know why I need to go back. I'm fine."

Roger tossed a glance over his shoulder. "You aren't fine. Blood is seeping through your bandage."

"Oh, York." Darcie straightened.

Despite her worry over him, she couldn't help but smile. He risked further damage to his arm to come for her. She'd never considered herself one of those sappy heroines from a B-rated romance movie, but his gesture created a warm fuzzy feeling as comfortable as a worn pair of slippers. Her smile faded when she spotted Pete's sedan parked in the center of the road.

"Stop the car. Don't let them see us." Darcie clutched his shoulder. "Pull over."

Roger steered until the squad car parked five hundred feet back and partially hidden beneath low hanging tree branches.

Maggie's pale face peered out the back window of Pete's car. Cigarette smoke created a grey cloud around her head. Another car pulled up and Richard Leroy climbed from the driver's seat, leaving his door open and the car running.

"That's him. That's Leroy." Darcie shrank back against York. "He can't see us, can he?"

"If he looks hard enough he will," Roger answered. "This white car won't hide against the green trees very well."

"Well, go get him." What was he waiting for? Darcie shoved at his shoulder.

"I'm not going without backup!"

Leroy pulled a gun from beneath his suit jacket and aimed it at Pete's car. The men's raised voices drifted to where Darcie and the others sat, but not clear enough for her to hear what they said. Was she going to watch as her mother was gunned down? Darcie couldn't swallow past the lump in her throat.

"Roger…"

"I see it." He unhooked his seatbelt and unsnapped the strap of leather holding his weapon in place. "Who's the woman?"

"My mother."

"What?" Roger whipped around so fast Darcie thought his head would fall off. "She's been with Leroy this entire time?"

Darcie shrugged. "I don't know, but she's with him now and he's holding a gun on her. She helped me escape, Roger. You've got to do something."

"If I wrote this, nobody would believe it." York ran a hand through his hair. "We're wasting time sitting here. Can't you shoot him and ask questions later?"

"In this circumstance, I guess I can. But it's going to make a lot of paperwork."

"Don't be so lazy." York smiled without humor.

"You sit behind a desk most of the time anyway. Now's your chance to be a hero."

Roger shoved open his door and stepped out. "Drop your weapon!"

Leroy spun and vaulted back into his car then sped away.

Roger sprinted to the other vehicle and ushered Pete and Maggie out. A siren wailed to a stop behind Roger's squad car.

"Now the cavalry arrives." York shifted beside her. "I've got to get out. Rigor-mortis is setting in."

"I'm sorry." Darcie scooted over. "There's no doorknob." She eyed Roger's open door through the screen dividing the front seat from the back. "We're stuck in here." She wiped perspiration from her upper lip and took a deep breath against her rising heartbeat.

"Hey." York clapped a hand on her shoulder. "You escaped from a gunfight, ran from an armed man, and you're afraid of being locked in a car? I'm here."

She took a deep, shuddering breath and wiped the perspiration from her face. "Confined spaces freak me out."

"Obviously." He placed a kiss on the top of her head. "Roger is coming back. He'll let us out."

"You know," Roger said as soon as he opened the back door. "I purposely didn't apply for law enforcement in a big city because I didn't want to deal with this kind of stuff. Darcie, your mother wants to speak with you."

"Okay." She gave York a shaky smile and headed up the road.

"Wait!" Roger slammed the door. "Don't go without me."

Darcie waved a hand at him. "Then you'd better hurry and catch up."

With an end to the nightmarish past few days coming to a close, Darcie increased her pace. Yes, her mother sat in the back of a police cruiser, but she'd helped Darcie escape. That earned her major points with her daughter.

Half-way to Darcie's destination, a car roared up and screeched to a halt beside her. She turned and looked into the barrel of Richard Leroy's gun. Her blood froze.

"Get in. Quickly."

# CHAPTER THIRTY-TWO

Darcie glanced back toward the squad car. York and Roger ran full speed toward her both of them clutching an arm to his side.

"Get in or I shoot one of them." Leroy grinned. "Possibly the man without a shirt?"

Darcie slid in.

He stepped on the gas before she had her door shut. Darcie craned her neck to look out the back window. Roger had his pistol aimed toward the speeding car. York held up a hand to stop him.

Leroy laughed. "Guess your man's afraid the cop might hit you instead of me. Smart guy."

"What do you want with me?" Darcie started to reach for her seatbelt then stopped. If she buckled in, she couldn't jump when the right situation presented itself. If nothing else, the last couple of days had taught her she wasn't the meek person she thought she was. The other thing she'd learned was that God provided opportunities. She needed to be ready to see and act upon them.

"I want the list your husband left."

"I don't have it."

He turned a steely, grey-eyed glare on her. "You'd better be able to obtain it then. Otherwise, you're no use to me."

Darcie gnawed her lower lip. How much time could she buy by taking Leroy to the Thayer's well? Would it be enough? Would York and Roger figure out where they'd gone? Her survival took on new meaning knowing that York lived. She cared what happened to her now.

"I thought you left." Darcie crossed her arms. "What did you want with Maggie? Why did you come back?"

"Your *mother* asked me not to kill you. Imagine my surprise with that revelation." He shrugged. "There's plenty of places to hide on these mountains. All I had to do was disappear over the next hill, turn around, and see what I could do. When I saw you between the two cars, I knew I had my chance." He laughed. "That cop really is stupid.

"All I need now is that list, and I'll be gone. Leave the country. Assume a new identity."

"Can't you do that now?"

"I don't like to leave loose ends, Mrs. Thayer." He tossed another glance her way. "Your husband should never have crossed me. Imagine my delight to hear about his death. Hire someone to fiddle with the brake line, and there you go."

Before she knew she would, Darcie hit him with her fist in the side of the head. "My baby died too!"

She continued to pummel him until he swerved the car, and she fell back. "For a year, I thought the accident had been my fault."

"I ought to shoot you now!" He waved the gun in her face. "Maggie's daughter or not. What do I care? Your mother's going to jail."

"Use them and throw them away, right?" Darcie straightened. "That's all people are to you. Well, *Mister* Richard Leroy, life has value. Enough value that God died for it. You want to shoot me then do it. Don't just sit there and wave your big gun around."

His eyes widened for a moment before a laugh burst from him. The strength of it made Darcie plaster herself against the door and reach for the handle poking into her back. "You got more backbone than your mother. I ought to keep you around for the entertainment." He tapped her leg with the barrel of his pistol. "Younger and prettier, too. I might enjoy the challenge of taming you."

Right. Like she'd let him.

She didn't know Roger very well, but she didn't think stupid was an apt description. He might be a small-town cop, but there might be more to the country man than Leroy gave him credit for. Plus, with York yapping at his heels, the man wouldn't be able to give up. Darcie smiled. She'd be all right.

"You should've asked Pete where the list is. He was there."

"What?" The car swerved again.

Darcie prayed her ploy would work. "He captured me, didn't he? *After* I found the envelope." She cringed at the man's string of curse words. He didn't need to know she didn't physically have the package when Pete ordered her into the car. If Leroy circled back…

"I can not believe this!" He pounded the steering wheel. Leroy whipped the car down a dirt road. "If Pete had it, he doesn't now. That means your cop friend does. You're the hostage I'll use to make an exchange."

"Give it up, Leroy." Darcie crossed her arms. "What does it matter now? They've seen the list. They've heard the tape by now…"

"Tape?"

Uh-oh. "You didn't know?"

"What's on it?"

She shrugged. "I didn't listen to it, but I'm guessing Tony spilled his guts. Between that and the infamous list, you'll have nowhere to hide."

"Shut up!"

Sweat ran down the man's crimson face. His slicked back hair fell loose from its pomade and flopped across his forehead. Fear and anger soured the air. She played with fire, and knew it. But rage sometimes made a person careless. She hoped it would Leroy.

"Where are we going?"

"I don't know." Spittle flew from his lips. "Be quiet and let me think. Why aren't you afraid? You ought to be cowering in the corner, crying."

Darcie tilted her head. "Why? My fate isn't in your hands. If you're going to kill me, nothing I do will stop you."

"You're crazy, do you know that?"

"Maybe." She stared out the window. Familiar

scenery bounced past them. Leroy headed toward her mother's old place then Darcie remembered.

"Uncle Dick." Darcie laughed. "You used to wear your hair longer and had a scruffy beard. You were one of mom's regulars."

"I was her last." They stopped in front of the ramshackle house. "I took her away from all this. Together, we made a fortune."

"By ill-gotten means." Darcie shoved her door open.

"By whatever way necessary." Keeping the gun aimed her direction, Leroy joined her. "Prostitution and drugs, at first. Then we moved up to giving out loans. That's where the real money is."

She turned to face him. "Now what?"

He handed her the cell phone from his pocket. "Call your friend. It's time to make a deal."

~

"Don't shoot, Roger. You might hit Darcie." York held up his hand.

"He's getting away."

"No. We figure out something else." York jogged to the car where Maggie smoked in the back seat. "Where would he take her?"

She exhaled. "The only place he knows around here is my old house. He won't kill her."

"Why not?"

"I asked him not to." A sad smile stretched Maggie's lips. "She's my daughter. As horrible a mother as I am, she's still that. And Richard loves me, as much as he is capable. He'll respect the one thing I've ever asked of him."

Hope leaped in York's heart. *Lord, let it be so.*

Roger joined him. "He's taking her to the old McGee place."

Roger frowned. "You sure?"

Maggie shrugged. "As sure as anything, I guess."

Roger slammed the door, locking her in with the hand-cuffed Pete. "Let's go." He climbed behind the wheel of his squad car while York dashed to the passenger side.

"He'll kill you if he sees you coming." Pete said. "He ain't nice like me."

York twisted in his seat. "Nice? You shot me!"

"Just doing my job. It was nothing personal."

"You and your friend killed Suzy."

"Again, just my job. Besides, Jack did it. I don't hit girls."

York took a deep breath against his rising anger. "Look, Leroy is no longer your boss. Roger is. Roger, give him an order."

"Shut up, Pete." Roger spun gravel taking them back to the road. He glanced in his rearview mirror. "Thank God. This is where you get out, Pete." Roger stopped the car and allowed the approaching cruiser to stop beside them.

He rolled down his window. "Got a passenger for you, boys."

"What about Maggie?" York inclined his head toward the back.

"We might still need her." Roger waited until the other officers switched Pete to their car, the man protesting the entire time against going to jail. Roger released a heavy sigh once he was gone. "It ain't personal," he muttered.

Maggie laughed; the sound so like Darcie's,

York turned to stare. He hadn't taken time to study the woman before. Beneath the thick makeup and over-processed hair, the resemblance between mother and daughter was striking.

She snorted as she tried to control her laughter. "The funny thing is, Pete really doesn't mean anything by what he does. He's a simple-minded man who does whatever Richard tells him. Except strike a woman." She shook her head. "I've never seen him do that. Richard, on the other hand, won't hesitate. I'd step on the gas if I were you, Mr. Cop."

York's blood ran cold. What horrors was Darcie facing? Her distrust of men left her moody and smart-mouthed. *Hold your tongue, Darcie. I'm coming.* His shoulder burned, his stomach growled, his head pounded, and over his discomfort hung the fear they'd be too late to save her.

# CHAPTER THIRTY-THREE

R oger's cell phone rang startling York and causing him to jerk.

The officer motioned his head toward the phone. "Get that would you. I'm going too fast to answer."

York grabbed the phone from the console and held it to Roger's ear. "This is Roger. Uh-huh. We'll be there in fifteen minutes." He glanced at York. "Leroy wants to exchange Darcie for the list."

"If he feels cornered, there's no telling what he'll do. He might not heed my request after all," Maggie said from the back seat. "Your best chance is for me to talk to him."

"How do I know you won't go into cahoots with him?" Roger glanced in his rearview mirror.

"You don't. But I'm the only chance you've got. Unless you have that list with you."

York glared at Roger. "Do you?"

Roger shook his head. "It's at the office, copied,

and distributed by now.”

“Great.” York slapped the dash board. “Now what?”

He’d never felt so helpless. Michelle’s death was the result of her own choices. Hopefully preventing Darcie’s was still in his hands and those of a cop who wanted nothing more than to lounge behind a desk in a small town and write the occasional speeding ticket.

As clearly as if God sat in the spoke from the seat next to him, York realized Darcie wasn’t in his human power to save. She was in God’s hands.

He wiped the tears from his eyes and stared out the window. Roger hadn’t handcuffed Maggie, and cigarette smoke drifted over the seat, stinging his nostrils. York glanced at Roger. He seemed deep in thought, then rolled down his window. The warm summer breeze grabbed the odor and whipped it from the cruiser. York expected Roger to tell the woman not to smoke but the man simply gripped the steering wheel and kept his gaze forward. A tell-tale stain of scarlet dotted the bandage around his left hand.

York glanced at the speedometer. Eighty miles per hour. He sent a prayer heavenward for their safety.

“I’m sorry.” Roger clenched his jaw.

“Excuse me?” York raised his gaze to the man’s face.

“For getting Darcie more involved than she was, for letting her away from my side, for not taking the shot when I should have, pick one.” Roger shrugged. “Until today, outside of the firing range,

I've never fired my weapon at anyone. I'm head of the department purely because of my knowledge of the law. Not necessarily my skill. Other officers have always been more than happy to take the risks."

"Do you hit your target at the range?" York asked.

"Every time. I'm a dead eye." Roger grinned. "Ironic, huh?"

"Boo-Hoo." Michelle slipped her cigarette butt through the wire mesh. "Be a dear and toss this, will you?"

"Put it out on the floor." Roger whipped the wheel to take the car down a dirt road. "Won't hurt it any and no more smoking. I'm about to gag. If I wanted smoking in the backseat, I would've installed an ash tray."

They bounced down a poorly-graded road. Roger smirked. "It might take longer than fifteen minutes on this road."

York ran a hand through his hair. If they were delayed, would Leroy think they weren't coming? Would he harm Darcie or leave? For the first time in his life, York wished for a gun to hold in his hand. One not intended for his annual deer hunting. The thought increased the acid burning in his stomach. If Leroy hurt Darcie, York didn't know what he'd do. Maybe it was a good thing he didn't have a weapon.

~

Leroy shoved his cell phone in his pocket and waved Darcie to a corner of the room. "Sorry, no furniture. You'll have to have a seat on the floor."

Darcie eyed the thick dust covering the warped board of the floor then glanced at the soiled shorts she wore. She shrugged and sat cross-legged in the corner.

A breeze would be nice. She lifted her hair off her neck.

Leroy paced like a fighter in a wrestling ring. His eyes flittered from her to the front window and back again. Through it all, he kept the gun trained on her. What did he think she could do? Wrestle him to the ground and take the pistol away? She wished.

"I'm thirsty."

Leroy glared. "Do I look like I have anything to drink?"

"What kind of a kidnapper are you, not having water for your captive?"

"A desperate one." His eyes squinted.

Honest enough. Darcie considered throwing dust in his face, but knew it was a futile attempt at best and would only anger the man. A stranger with a gun wasn't someone she wanted to enrage. She sighed.

"Where are they?" Leroy glanced at his watch. "Can't people be on time?" His face reddened.

"They'll be here as soon as they can." Darcie started to rise and changed her mind when he gave her another stern look. She ought to be frightened, but amazingly enough, she felt only peace.

"What are you smiling about?" Leroy stopped pacing. "I could shoot you now and be done with it."

"You could." Darcie stretched her legs in front of her. "I was thinking about God. Really haven't spent much time over the years doing that. Better late than never, don't you think?"

Leroy snorted. "I've heard the news reports about the occasional victim who converts their captor. Don't waste your breath. I've heard it all."

Darcie opened her mouth to argue, then snapped it closed. Who was she? Just days ago she'd basically said the same thing to York. If he hadn't ordered her to read the Bible, would she have? She honestly didn't know. Now, she sat in inch-thick dust under the watchful eye of a frantic madman waiting for rescue to ride in at dusk. Only God kept her from becoming a quivering mass of tears.

A car crunched up the driveway. Leroy grabbed Darcie's arm and yanked her to her feet. With one arm across her neck and the other poking the gun into her back, he scooted them through the front door opening and onto the sagging porch.

York bolted from the car.

"Hold it right there, lover boy." Leroy tightened his grip. "Unless you want to see what color this pretty girl's blood is."

York's face paled. Roger stepped from the car and opened the door for Maggie. She moved ahead of him and posed seductively against the front bumper.

"Now, Richard, sweetie, you don't want to do this." She fumbled down her shirt for a cigarette, spoiling the vision of seductress. Darcie smiled. Maggie might look polished, but she still acted enough like the mother she knew. She'd use all her feminine wiles to get what she wanted, and the ever present smoke would give her courage.

"Come over here, Maggie."

She shook her head. "I'm sorry, but this is one time I can't do what you want. I'm in custody of the police, and you're holding my only child at gunpoint." Her hand shook as she raised her lighter.

"I've never asked anything from you. Not even the clothes on my back. You've showered me with gifts," She paused to take a puff. "And I appreciate every one of them. We've had a good life, Richard. But you've got to let my girl go."

Darcie's heart warmed. She couldn't remember her mother ever calling her "her girl", darling, or any of the other sentiments children grew up hearing. The slight tremors in her mother's hands told Darcie of the woman's nerves. Despite her words, Leroy didn't lighten his grip.

"I want the list. This girl said she gave it to Pete."

Roger and York glanced at each other, then Roger took a step forward. "Then Pete gave it to me. It's at the station. There's nothing I can do. The information is out now."

Leroy moved the gun's barrel to Darcie's temple. "Then we're at a standoff, gentlemen. I'll take this little lady, and Maggie, and we'll go. Once we're away, I'll let this one loose."

Roger shook his head. "I can't let you do that."

"What are you doing?" York whipped his gaze from Darcie to Roger.

"I can make the shot, York."

"No."

Leroy laughed. "Listen to him, copper man. He's got a brain in his head."

Maggie dropped her cigarette and ground it into the dirt with her stiletto heel. "This is ridiculous. Richard, let her go. Hire a lawyer, and we'll put an end to all this. If you kill her, no amount of money will get you out of jail."

"After all I've done for you, you've turned against me." His hold tightened more on Darcie's throat, and she squirmed for air. Leroy raised his arm, forcing her head back. He lifted Darcie until only her toes touched the wood beneath her.

Through tunnel vision, she made out the faces of those watching. "Take the shot." She forced the words through her tortured throat. She cupped her hands around her neck and breathed in and out slowly.

Maggie took two more steps forward. She stretched a hand toward Darcie. "You're choking her, Richard."

"I'm aware of that!" He dragged Darcie back into the cabin and threw her to the floor. "They'll be coming. There's no door to keep them out."

"I'm sorry. It fell off the hinges when I opened it a few days ago." Swallowing was a burning torture. Every breath wheezed through her esophagus, forcing its way through bruised muscle.

Leroy's hand shook as he aimed the gun at her. "If they do, you'll be the first one to fall under a bullet. Tell them to stay outside."

"York, Roger, stay there! He'll shoot if you come." The effort to shout brought tears to her eyes. There had to be a way out of this madness. Darcie glanced frantically around the room. A splintered two-by-four lay a few feet from her. If she could distract him long enough…

"Richard." Maggie appeared in the doorway. "I'm here. I would never desert you."

Leroy turned his attention away from Darcie. She crawled across the floor.

He started to turn back in her direction. His gun hand raised.

Darcie grabbed the board and swung at the back of his legs.

He fell to his knees.

She scrambled to wrench the gun from his hands. Rising to her feet, chest heaving, she leveled the weapon at him. She couldn't prevent the momentary smile that spread across her face. She'd done it. Instead of cowering beneath the weight of fear, she had taken the initiative and saved herself.

"Mom," she said without turning. "Please let Roger and York know they can come in."

"Don't hurt him. Regardless of his crimes, I love him."

"I won't hurt him."

Leroy glared at Darcie from the floor. "Shoot me. I don't want to go to jail."

"We don't always get what we want. But we often get what we need. Think about turning your life around while you're behind bars. It'll be the best decision you ever make." Her hand shook as she giggled at the recitation of a song lyric. Her newfound faith, and the strength that accompanied it, made her a new woman. For the first time in a long time, she looked forward to the future.

Roger dashed to her side and gently took the gun from her hand. "I'll take it from here."

Darcie stepped back into York's waiting arms. He wrapped her close with his uninjured one and kissed the top of her head. Roger handcuffed the fallen Richard Leroy and shoved him out the door.

Darcie turned into York. "Now what, Mr. York?"

"Now, I teach you how to live." He lowered his head.

The End

Scan this code to learn more about Collision Course

# ABOUT THE AUTHOR

www.cynthiahickey.com

Cynthia Hickey is a multi-published and best-selling author of cozy mysteries and romantic suspense. She has taught writing at many conferences and small writing retreats. She and her husband run the publishing press, Winged Publications. They live in Arizona and Arkansas, becoming snowbirds with three dogs. They have ten grandchildren who keep them busy and tell everyone they know that "Nana is a writer."